The Tales My Wrinkles Tell

The Tales My Wrinkles Tell

Dr. Krishna Saksena

Ocean Paperbacks

A Division of Ocean Books Pvt. Ltd.

ISO 9001:2008 Publishers

Published by
Ocean Paperbacks
A Division of Ocean Books Pvt. Ltd.
4/19 Asaf Ali Road,
New Delhi-110 002 (INDIA)
e-mail: info@oceanbooks.in

ISBN 978-81-8430-296-7
The Tales My Wrinkles Tell
by Dr. Krishna Saksena

Edition
First, 2014

Price
Rs. 150.00 (Rs. One Hundred Fifty only)

Printed at
Bhanu Printers, Delhi

Introduction

The author, crossing 86 years of her life, looks back through the mist of time. There were timeless moments when she walked out in her youth, finding every day an awakening. Those were simple days, of simple people, few rules yet great achievements. She recounts those incidents that still stand sharp in her memory, people she cannot forget, happenings that show her the way and give shape to her philosophy of life. Interesting incidents and peculiar personalities are sure to catch the attention of all those who go through this book and see the difference between how things are today and how they were not long ago.

Preface

Dr. Krishna Saksena's latest book "The Tales my Wrinkles Tell" is a wonderful collection of stories, reminiscences and discourses, very readable and containing wisdom acquired over a lifetime. Some of the stories are about Priti, a thoughtful young girl and her family of six sisters, in which the author revisits her past and derives some valuable lessons from her experiences. In others, Priti enters into a dialogue with her wise neighbour, Mrs.Vadvani, who expounds her views about the meaning and purpose of life, about God, religion, bhakti, and righteous living, but throughout the author maintains a light touch which keeps the interest of the readers alive. It is a book which teaches while it entertains and explores spiritual concepts in simple language.

– Dr. Rajul Sogani
Professor Delhi University

Contents

Not Long Ago

(In the city of Lucknow, year 1945)

It was a locality where people from varied professions lived happily with their families. A doctor, an inspector, a manager of a private company, professors and few others like businessmen and senior retired officials lived close to each other. All had children. Some had more sons than daughters, while others had more daughters than sons. Children were considered as blessings by their parents, though they may be many in numbers. There existed a close communion amongst them all. They were together in each other's rejoicings and sorrows. If elders found little time to meet each other, the children made it up on the playground. They believed in the goodness of all. They understood the problems and feelings of each other. When at times the occasion arose they always stood behind each other.

The approach of the early hours of the morning was announced by the shrill voice coming out of the mosque of the locality. It sounded together with the jingling of bells from the temple nearby. But from the doctor's house the sweet music of a bhajan sung in a very emotional voice accompanied by a guitar raised the spirit of all those who heard it. These were signals sure enough that the time had come when all must get up, remember God and begin their daily routine. But the little ones in the house of the professor of an intermediate college waited for another signal to get up. They needed another closer and loving signal, the call of their mother. The professor, Dr. Lal was a diminutive character, but a distinguished man, a prominent educationist who spoke softly but firmly. When he spoke, people listened to him. In contrast to this Baba was Amma, his wife, always at the highest pitch of her voice. She was a bundle of frantic energy who would come in like a whirlwind and would leave in her wake people reeling and scrambling.

"Get up fast. It is getting late. You little ones how is it that you are still sleeping?" They were eight in number, two brothers and six sisters. All lights were switched on as in other houses of the locality. There was commotion all round. The mother started pulling up the sheets with which they had covered themselves. All types of excuses were ready, "I am tired", said one, while the other explained, "You know Amma, I slept very late, so I need to sleep a little longer," the next made a sick face and said, "I am a little feverish". The mother shouted, "No excuses, get up fast". This made them all sit up in their beds rubbing their eyes with both their hands and finally getting ready to jump out of their beds.

Bihari, the servant boy, who slept on the ground downstairs, was no better. The mother went up to him and shouted, "It is getting very late and the children have to go to school, so get up fast". "Oh no, it is still dark and too early to get up". The mother had to lower her voice and explain, "You know, Bihari, the hot jalaibies in the shop would all be sold out, and then there would be nothing there for you for the breakfast". For Bihari it was a temptation too difficult to resist, so fast he got up, folded his mat and ran to start his work.

The house of the professor was a three storied building, and during summers all the members of the house preferred to sleep on the top floor. The other houses of the locality also had three stories. They all loved the openness and the fresh air that was there during the night and early morning. They were refreshed by the cool breeze that gave them new vigour needed for the tasks of the coming day.

There were only two toilettes and two bathrooms, one set on the first floor and one on the second floor. So the children on getting up ran fast to be the first ones to occupy the toilets. Others had to form a queue. Cries rose from all directions. The children were shouting, and making lot of noise,

"Have you gone off to sleep that you are taking so much time sitting inside", Kamla shouted. She complained to the mother who happened to pass that side. The mother said "Come out fast dear" as she walked off busy in her own errands. "Just wait for a few seconds. I am coming out fast" Sarla replied. The same noise was there on the ground floor. The mother had to leave her work and go there. The same queue was there before the bathroom. She spoke a little annoyed, "Why are you shouting, dear child". "I have been waiting here for the last fifteen minutes. You could have allowed me to sleep a little longer than waste my time here" said Poonam. The mother replied calmly, "Why waste time, you can in the meantime go and pack your bag. Your teacher has complained that you often forget to bring your books". "I know, Amma, you will always take the side of this girl as against me" said Poonam very much annoyed with her mother. The mother only smiled back mischievously and went off. So taking their turns fast the entire circle was ready to move on.

The eldest was a boy Kanhaiya, handsome, healthy, and unpresuming. He was followed by four sisters Priti, proud and talkative, Kamla, beautiful and quiet, Subhasha, plain and submissive, Sarla, simple and adjusting. Sarla was considered lucky for the family as a son was born after her. There was great rejoicing on his birth, as he came 'most wanted'. Sarla got loving pats on her back for she brought happiness to the family. The boy was named Narayan. He grew up very naughty, difficult and talkative. He was followed again by two sisters Poonam, strong in her views and egoistic and Mannorama, very sweet and always smiling. Then there were few other cousin sisters and brothers with various qualities that had to join this group now and then as there were little facilities of education in their villages. The mother being a mother loved all her children, both daughters and sons. But in particular she was partial to her sons. Her sons meant a lot to her. They were her pride, for in the future life they would carry her name and promised support. Before going to bed, she would make sure that they got their share of *malai,* which the daughters did not get. The father had no such inhibitions, for him all were alike. They were all his assets, daughters as well as sons. He made no difference between them. All were equally his pride. He was sure that they would all fulfill his ambitions.

After taking bath, they entered the Puja room and stood in a line. The father at this time would come and speak lovingly to his children, "Look here, my little ones, this house is a temple". Poonam tried to correct him, "No, Baba, the temple is a little far away from here". "No, my dear little child, it is you who will account for the holiness of this place by your actions of love, understanding and faith. It is this holiness alone that will make this house a temple". Children did not understand much what Baba meant but preferred to keep quiet. Baba continued, "To make it simple for you if you are good to each other, if you love one other and are helpful to every one around you, happiness will be here all round. This house will then become a temple". "I see" remarked Priti, thoughtfully and assured her father, "Baba, we shall all try to move in the direction shown by you". Others also nodded. "All right, now fold your hands and close your eyes", the father said. "Be ready to recite your mantra and pray God to give you the courage to be good to others and to be good to yourself". The children obeyed. The father then told the children to go and take their breakfast and run to school.

Bihari, the servant boy, had already brought hot jalebies from the market. Mother gave each child a glass of milk

with four jalebies. After taking their breakfast they ran to their rooms to pack up their bags. Before moving out kamla reminded her mother, "Amma, you are forgetting something very important".
"What is that?" she asked anxiously.
"Our daily wages for studying hard" replied Sarla in a serious tone.
Amma smiled back mischievously as she opened the knot of her saree palloo and distributed two paisa to each child. She, however, warned, "Be careful that you eat something clean and good".
"Sure, sure", the children shouted as they ran out.

Tonga was ready to take them to school. They all sat down. Abdulla, the tonga-wala started off with a loud voice and a swing of his whip. The horse ran, bells tied to his neck jingled. There rose out of this sound a sweet music that told the little children that they must begin the day with enthusiasm to study with earnestness. If any student was seen on the road walking, the children would stop the 'tonga' and she would quickly jump into it. There was no feeling of obliging or being obliged. It was just a very natural feeling of concern for each other. It came naturally. Such training was given to the children at home and at school. The whole vicinity was a place where simplicity of hearts was a common feature. The 'tonga' stopped at the gate of the school and the children ran out fast.

The schools were not co-eds. Boys and girls studied separately. The children went to a missionary school, aided by Americans. The teaching methods were really good. There was strict discipline. There existed a close relationship between the teacher and the taught. Some slight punishment was allowed when children went the wrong way or did not behave well. It was never hard, only good enough to make a student realize that she or he had gone a wrong way and therefore must take steps to correct.

The teacher took great interest in those whom she taught. She was responsible for them. Once Priti brought a complaint notice from the Principal that she was not up to the mark in Mathematics and was a little behind the class, which should be made up by some help at home. Her Baba replied, "Ever since I have put my child under your care I have felt always free and confident, because I knew I had transferred my responsibility to competent and caring hands". The Principal was much impressed by the remark and arranged for an extra class, where the teacher brought Priti up to the mark. When the children walked out of school, they could write and speak correct English and were pretty well versed in other subjects too. They had learnt the lesson of self confidence. It gave them the strength to keep on looking for new directions and to new lessons that they needed to learn, which surely is what life is all about. It was taught to them that they needed to be lamps to themselves and to be their own refuge. They were taught to strive and never to give up.

All went to school except Amma's darling Narayan. He hated being bound to a place for a long time. Twice he was admitted and twice his name was struck off the rolls because of his absence. The school appeared to him like a jail and he had committed no wrong to be there. Like a free deer he would run from one place to another, playing with marbles, flying kites or telling jokes. He had grown ten years old, not willing to go to school or to sit down to study. All round efforts failed. Had it been a daughter the mother would have allowed her to go her way as for the girls, marriage was the goal. But here a son was in question. It was left to Amma to put him on the track. How could she leave her darling son in that state? She pondered for a good long time looking to every one for help, but finally not finding any help she thought of a trick. She told Narayan,

"Look here, my child, I have stopped your pocket money because you refused to go to school".

"Too bad on your part, Amma".

"Yes, but I think I can give you one anna instead of two paisa only if you start studying. I will teach you for an hour all important subjects. But then you will sit down for another hour and finish all the work that I will give you. As soon as this is finished you can have your anna and your way".

"Agreed, I shall do as you say, but I must have my anna the minute I finish my work".

"Agreed" said the mother.

The attraction of one anna was too great for Narayan. He jumped with joy as the mother continued, "You know well that I never make false promises".

So the deal was made and from the next day the work started. Poor mother had to take out one hour from her busy schedule of house jobs as he would not study from any one else.

For one hour the mother taught and then gave him enough work to occupy him for another hour. She would then go to the toilet. Before going away the mother said, "I am going to the toilet. Try to finish by the time I come out, because only then you will get your money". Narayan started doing his work fast. He finished it in half an hour. He closed his note book, over it he put the pen and safely kept it on the table and ran towards the toilet where his mother was still there and shouted, jumping all the time with impatience "Amma I have finished the work, give my anna fast".

"But I am in the toilet; I will give you as soon as I come out".

"Nothing doing, I cannot wait a minute longer. You can slightly open the door and throw the money out from there. If you forget your promise the deal will be over". Narayan warned, "No studying from tomorrow".

"Oh no" Amma sighed in despair, timidly got up from the pot, took an anna out from her knotted palloo, slightly opened the door and threw the anna out".

Narayan who was all the time jumping with impatience gave a still higher jump in sheer joy, ran, picked up the money and went out fast.

The mother when she came out checked his work and found that all was done correctly. She was quite surprised that the work was completed in so short a time. Encouraged she continued teaching him for six months. He was good enough to take an entrance exam for the sixth class. But he refused to go to school and said to his mother,

"Amma you are a good teacher and I will continue learning from you all my life".

Poor mother! She did not know what to do. She thought for sometime and then said "Look here my child I will give you two annas if you promise to go to school". "The deal is not bad, Amma" replied Narayan, after some serious thinking, "I will try as you do not have time to teach me".

So the next day, putting two annas in his pocket, he went to school and appeared for class sixth examination and qualified. He started going to school and his teacher applauded him for his good work. It made him easy to sit in the class. When result came out he was at the top of the class. The father was really happy at the achievement the mother had made especially when Narayan was declared a gone case by all. He was always the best boy of the class, leaving far behind all those who had joined the school from K.G. But he made sure that he had two annas in his pocket before he left for school.

On returning from school, all sat down for lunch. A carpet was spread out on the floor where all sat down. A thali with small bowls containing dal, vegetables, chapaties, rice and chatni was brought in. All sat in a circle around it and took their food. Their happiness was in eating good, healthy and simple food, which they enjoyed. They laughed, cracked jokes, and told each other what happened in their classes and were happy. They also fought sometimes but soon made up forgot easily and forgave fast.

Togetherness was the essence of their existence from which came a feeling of oneness. Together they were with their neighbours and friends. Together they were on the playground. Together they sat down to study. Together they huddled down in their beds at night to hear the stories from their Nani narrated in her inimitable way. Together they would fall off to sleep and they rose in the morning together to run and start their work of the day. There came out a harmonious tone in their lives when they played together with their friends and neighbours, when they shouted together with others and when they studied together in school or at home. No one was a stranger and there rose a loud symphony from them that "the entire world belongs to us". They were fully satisfied as they smiled and blossomed like flowers and every one benefited from the peace that came out of it.

They were fully satisfied with whatever they got. Simple amusements were good enough for the children. The man on the street walking with two ropes in his hand, each tied round the necks of two monkeys, one female and one male. In the other hand he held a *dugdugi* with which he made a loud sound and announced that he had come to show the monkeys' dance drama. The children would pester Amma to give them money to see the show. Sometimes she would agree and children would run to call their friends in the neighbourhood. The spirit to share their joys with others was intense and nothing could be enjoyed alone. This was a common feature amongst all in the vicinity. All stood in a circle and the man with a loud sound made by his *dugdogi* started the dance drama of the two monkeys. At the end he would make one monkey go round and beg for money. The children would clap, jump and laugh together enjoying every moment of the show.

The other show was that of the cinemascope. A man would carry a big box on his shoulders which contained photographs of great interest that he would show by turning a handle and at the same time singing, telling about the picture that was before them. "Here goes the queen" he sang in his loud melodious voice, as he started to roll the handle, "Watch carefully the jewel in her crown and now comes the Taj, a beautiful place to see ...". Inside there was complete darkness and the children could see the images only through holes. There was light on the images. The man carried a bell, which he rang as he sang and told them stories about those images. The children were thrilled. Few paisa spent and so much amusement!!

More interesting than these were the parties that would arrive at the vicinity and staged their shows. They would select some central ground where they enacted episodes from Ramayan and Bhagvatam. Here the elders joined the youngsters and the scenes like Sita Swayamber or Krishna Leela were enacted. These were very much liked and highly appreciated by all. This was absolutely free.

But the best was when, during summer vacations the children came together and enacted full fledged dramas. Tickets were sold. The hall of a nearby school was taken on request from the authorities. The elders who came to see, applauded and gave encouragement to the children. In the end with whatever money they made they sat feasting, laughing, and enjoying themselves. So the holidays were never allowed to be dull.

The first radio in the house of Kamla came as a wonder. The sisters in their enthusiasm went about calling their friends and neighbours to come to hear the programmes on it. Here was something new. The whole room would be full and that pleased them. If, however some one did not turn up Priti would run to see what the reason was. Such was the concern for each other. Their little world was so simple, so beautiful.

So the six sisters and two brothers grew up well fulfilling the ambition of their father. They were brilliant students getting only first division in their classes. When Priti's photograph was flashed in all the papers, both English and Hindi, for excelling in her subject, which was English, it made the father so proud. He went about showing the paper to all his neighbours and to all his friends. It carried the line- "She is the daughter of an educationist". The gleam in his eyes showed how the daughter was no different from a son. If someone asked him, "You never think how you will marry so many daughters?" His answer was always there with a winning smile, "Well, they will go where they are destined to. Why should I bother about their marriage?" My work is to give them education and a right direction to follow in their lives emphasizing on the best values that need to be inculcated". Others would marvel at the ease with which he spoke. He was always calm.

The first marriage in the vicinity was that of Kanha, who had become a lawyer. It was an auspicious occasion to be celebrated by all. There were no discos, no decorations and no 'pandals'. Only the front verandah from where the new-comer would enter the house was cleaned up and a few flowers and garlands put here and there. The six sisters with their friends from the neighbourhood joined to form the orchestra. One who was an expert in sitar sat with her sitar. The other with a flute was ready to play on it. The tabla girl sat in the middle and the one with harmonium was in no way willing to sit behind. Those with lovely sweet voices stood up in the front to sing the welcome song, a song composed by those among them who had the poetic talent. Few were ready to clap while others held the garlands in the hands. It was an occasion which had the participation of all. They were ready to start the music simultaneously waiting, holding their breath. The car carrying the bride stopped. She was covered all over by a gorgeous sari. A glamorous 'dupatta' on her head covered half her face. Her fingers had shining diamond rings while her arms were full of golden bangles. As she moved towards the veranda the atmosphere was filled up by the melodious sound of all the instruments. It went up high and echoed in the entire locality. As she came near the gate the flowers were showered on her. She was made to wait, garlanded and then the lovely sweet tune of the welcome song filled the atmosphere.

"O dear Bhabhi, we welcome you to your new home,
Our hearts are full of joy, we are thrilled as you join us
We all unite and a song we sing: Welcome, welcome,
Our most loving Bhabhi, we all love you".

It was so touching that all those who watched stood dumb. The music and the sound of the orchestra that accompanied it filled the air and spread all over. When the song was over, the bride slowly walked inside. Such were the ways to celebrate the special occasions. So simple yet heart warming. A celebration joined by all that went deep into the very souls of those who watched.

Children grew up and moved together with understanding and caring for all. There was no need to give them lectures on compassion and on concern. These came automatically and were rooted in their hearts and minds. It was then very easy to move on gracefully with all. If any one needed help they came running forward. Together they grew up rejoicing in the best of times and consoling others in the worst of times.

And this was not long ago. Can you believe this?

□

Politics and the Professor

Don't you think that without stories, we would go mad? Stories can achieve that which we have never dreamt of. Stories can conquer fear and tell you how you need to handle any problem. Stories real or false mean a lot. If you do not know the stories you may feel lost in life. So here is another story in the life of the professor's family with six daughters, Priti leading them all.

A strange man, Shibban Lal Saxena, was a constant figure who visited the family off and on. Tall, stout and heavy, he had a prominent personality by his very make up. His position as a founder leader of a prominent party K.M.P (Kisan Mazdoor Praja party) made him still taller. He would enter the house of the Professor, climb up the stairs, leaving his followers downstairs. He was greatly respected by all. His frequent visits brought him closer to the family. He was addressed by the six as Mama. They called their dear mother as Amma and she did not mind such a towering personality to become her brother though he was related to her in a very distant way. Shibban ji showed himself to be very close to this dear sister, so a great well wisher of this family.

He would come twice a week, almost shaking the stairs by his weight and creating a noise by his might. All were seen on their toes. They would run to offer him a seat where he sat with great confidence and looked around. His political party at that time was at the height of popularity and men considered it their good luck if they got enrolled in it. Amma with all her six children would sit with him to hear what he had to say.

"You know Ram Hari Babu?" asked Shibban. Amma would nod her head and others would lend their ears so as not to miss any part of what he had to tell.

"I made him the man that he is now", said Shibban.

"How?" Amma would ask innocently.

"By bringing him into my party, and making him contest elections. You know he was elected only because of me and ever since then he has moved up in society and you can see for yourself how he is prospering today".

Amma would nod her head in sheer acceptance of what he said and would ask,

"Would you like to have your lunch here". For that was the only way that she could extend honour to her famous brother.

"Yes, of course, it is lunch time. I am very hungry. I know you are an expert in cooking. I am eager to have my lunch here".

Amma well pleased would run to the kitchen to decorate his plates with her best preparations. Shibban ji would then tell Priti,

"Two are sitting downstairs and you need to send them food also".

Priti would run to Amma to give her this message,

"Mama wants that food should also be sent for those sitting downstairs".

This became a regular feature in the family of the Professor. Shibban would come thumping on the stairs, enjoy a sumptuous lunch readily given by his sister and then would entice all by narrating a new story, that he had made up.

"You know, sister, our relative Pappu?" Shibban would ask.

"I know him very well", Amma replied.

"I made him what he is now". Shibban took all the credit to himself every time he narrated a new story.

"I made him contest the election. I got him elected. He is having a very good time for the last few years and has saved enough for the future. If you have any doubts you can ask him whenever you meet him."

Amma's imagination went high as he told his sister to ask her husband to contest in the coming elections. A simple lady that Amma was, she got caught up by her brother's clever device to attract her to his plans that he had in his mind to get regular lunch for himself and for his followers. Shibban would sit and advise his sister,

"You are limiting yourself. Don't do that. Many people limit themselves to what they think they can do. You can go far if your mind lets you go. You can achieve what you believe in. If opportunities come they need to be taken and immediately grasped".

"You know, brother, Amma would reply in her simple way, "I have grave responsibilities before me and I cannot take to your ideas that sound so strange to me. From a simple and a satisfied life of an ordinary person I cannot jump to the heights of your political world of high ambitions".

He then narrated more stories, about so many of those who acted on his advice. She wavered but deep within her self there was something that was stirring her up to take up the challenge. It was hope, a feeling to realize her dream to rise high in life. It gave her courage to endure and attempt anything whatsoever to rise high. She felt strongly that here was a challenge to test her courage and willingness to change. The challenge could not wait and she must act promptly. She was ready to accept the challenge, a struggle that would make her realize her dream. Life is all about facing challenges if one has to rise. At times she wavered, but soon the dreams that she saw were tempting and attractive. What if her husband became an M.P? Her brother's protection was there. Soon her family would occupy a high position which would greatly help her in marrying her six daughters. All would prosper. So hope and dreams moved her which soon conquered her doubts and fears. The conflict was over and she was ready for any risk.

"You have to fear nothing if I am by your side. Where I stand victory is assured. The question of defeat has no place. The Professor has only to fight election in my constituency. The responsibility of making him an M.P is mine. You do not know that I am the uncrowned king of my area. All those I sponsor must win the battle".

Such assurances given to the simple lady as Amma by her clever brother carried her off her feet. She was lead into her dreams which she saw coming true. Soon doubts started dwindling off and she felt strongly that there was no harm in following her brother. It now became Amma's duty to convince all around her specially Baba who never came in contact with Shibban. It was essential for her to include all in the dreams that moved her. It is only when there is all round support that management can work wonderfully well. Lives become beautiful if all are included as part of dream management. She moved and convinced her husband as well her children that the step to enter politics would definitely enrich their lives. She succeeded and all were enthusiastic to undertake this hazardous mission. Amma's dream was sure to come true as she took all with her. Their world would entirely change with better position, more money and a life of prosperity. All sang the same tune as Amma. Intoxicated with the dream of a better future they refused to hear any one who created the least doubt. Not willing to accept their error that they were going to tread a wrong path they brushed aside all such hints and argued, "They are jealous of our becoming prominent in society".

The entire family was happy at the thought that they would soon rise high in status and position. They would soon be counted amongst the prosperous. Amma was confident and Baba pretty sure that best days were ahead. The six children joined them in their expectations. All round the joy bells rang loudly.

So, full of enthusiasm from all sides, Baba went to file his nomination papers. A small truck was brought into service with a driver, who belonged to the area of his constituency. Enough money was taken for petrol and personal needs on the way. All the children were busy with their schools. It was only Priti who was free. She had finished her M.A and was contemplating which direction she should move next. So Baba for support asked Priti,

"Would you like to come with me and help me out in canvassing?"

"If Amma has no problem in my going out and helping you I am ready", replied Priti.

For Amma, nothing could block her way to achieve her dream. She readily agreed. So Baba and Priti moved on their path with one vision before them that soon they would be great.

The truck started. Baba and Priti kept on waving their hands constantly and vehemently with faces full of smiles till they lost the sight of those whom they had left. From the moment they stepped out they were expected to perform. How they played their innings in the political arena was left to them entirely.

The first landing was at the principal town of their constituency namely Deoria. No one recognized the Professor. His language was quite different from theirs. But he could manage to follow it with some difficulty. The people could follow him with a lot of strain. But the confidence that he would soon become their representative gave him an assurance that the problem would be resolved. They understood each others language to a great extent and it was more than enough for them to proceed with hopes of success.

Priti opened the chart to see the route they had to follow. After taking lunch, they started. They had to cross some area during the night to reach the village of Sanari in the morning, an appropriate time to address the villagers. It was about to get dark when they came near to cross this area. One man was seen running towards them giving them desperately a signal to stop. When he came near he asked Baba,

"Where are you going at this time?"

"I intend to cross this area, in which we have landed, during the night and arrive at Sonali by morning to start my canvassing campaign".

"What?" he looked quite surprised. He then continued. "It seems you do not know that this remote village which you are going to cross at night is the worst and well known criminal area of this constituency. You will be beaten, looted and thrown out. And this young girl whom you are taking with you will be abducted. You will not be left in a state to carry on your mission. You seem to be an outsider. Turn your car this very minute. Good luck to you that I met you. The criminals become active as soon it begins to get dark. Still there is time, so go back and begin your work when the day breaks."

Then he turned to the driver and scolded him in his own dialect "Are you conspiring with the criminals? You belong to this place and you could have well advised them not to take such a step".

"I told them but they insisted on following their time schedule. I was helpless" the driver replied.

"Now right away turn your truck back and drive them out of this danger zone, which you have entered. Drive at a very fast speed to carry them out of this criminal area in the shortest time that you have".

Baba said to Priti "I hope he is not making a fool of us".

"Why should he do that?" A shiver ran through her body when she heard the gentleman. So she insisted "Let us turn back, before it gets too late and do what the gentleman has told us. We need to avoid any catastrophe right at the start of our mission".
Baba then ordered the driver to turn back. He drove at a very high speed to be out of the place before the darkness enveloped them.

Early in the morning, when there was enough light they started. The criminals had gone off to sleep after their busy night. They arrived at Sanari a little late when the farmers and workers and the labourers had finished their lunch. Without stopping to take their lunch, they started on their mission. Priti played the record on the gramophone and put the speaker on it. The song went too far and wide. People, men, women and children all came running and stood before the truck. Priti came out to address them. Taken aback that a young girl was going to speak to them, they heard her in silence. Baba stood by her to watch the reaction of the crowd. Priti began,

"My Baba is here to ask you for your support in the coming elections. He belongs to the very popular party of farmers and labourers, Kisan Mazdoor Praja party, a party with a difference. It stands to take care of all your concerns, interest; free loans, free education, electricity and many other things that you may require from time to time. If you vote for him, he promises that he willa leave no stone unturned to get you all that you aspire for".

A loud cheer from the people followed as they clapped with great enthusiasm. Baba was happy that Priti had made a good impression on the crowd.
"You have done a good job" said Baba
"I will do my very best" assured Priti
"Sure we will succeed" said Baba. Priti smiled back

They moved on to their next village, Garail. Luckily it was the mela day. People from small neighboring villages had gathered there to do their purchasing. Animals stood there to be sold. At various places all types of grain was heaped. Clothes typical of the village taste were there. A lot of activities were going on all around. Priti told Baba,
"I am feeling nervous as the crowd is too heavy. It is better that you speak here".
So Baba got down, while Priti played a song very popular with the villagers. It amused many and attracted all. There was a huge gathering that stood before the truck. Priti stopped the music and Baba got down to speak. The crowd was very attentive to Baba as he spoke in his inimitable way.

"We the farmers and the labourers look and hope for a better life after independence. Your desires and inspirations are similar to mine as I too come from a farmer's family. I am here to represent your case to the government. I will try my best to fulfill your ambitions and enable you to lead a happy satisfied life. So I seek your support. I represent the K.M.P. Please cast your valuable vote for me as I wish to work for you, for your family and for your children".

There was a loud applause from the public, which greeted him warmly saying
"We shall all vote for you".
Baba bowed as he went to sit inside the truck.
The crowd dispersed as the truck moved on. Priti gave a further boost to his Baba's spirit by saying, "Excellent work done".

Mama Shibban had assured of his presence during this time. He had told his sister that he was the uncrowned king of this constituency and his presence once would assure Baba his victory. But ever since Baba and Priti had gone on their canvassing expedition, he forgot his sister and all those who ran to serve him. Repeated requests were sent to his office by his sister,
"Shibban Ji, as desired by you, my husband has gone for canvassing in the constituency allotted by you. He has been there for a pretty long time but you have failed to make your appearance as promised. We are working on your advice but there has been no response from your side. I am sure soon you will get time to go there and be true to your word".
There was absolutely no response, only his followers answered,
"The leader is too busy at the moment, but on finding time he will definitely consider going to the Professor's constituency".
Hopes lingered as time passed on. Priti's heart sank but the large crowds they attracted gave sustenance to their hopes.

In the next village of Sonda, Priti was quite surprised to see large crowds of women that gathered with men around the truck. Priti was clever enough to choose the right song suiting the place. After finishing her speech, which the crowd heard in rapt attention, women came close to her and said,

"We are baffled when we look at you. We would like you to answer one question that all of us have for you".

"And what is that?" Priti asked.

"Are you a girl or a boy?" they spoke together.

Poor Priti did not know how to answer this difficult question. She was very thin and delicate and besides it she was putting on a coat as it was winter. It amused Priti as she answered back smiling,

"I am what you make me out".

Saying so she sat in the truck and moved on. Often, poor thing, she was much harassed by the goonda element in some of the villages and she wished that she had not come. But then she gathered her strength to face all such situations with tact.

Sarla, Priti's sister assisted her in this tedious job for sometime. They moved together on foot from one cluster of huts to another. In one such cluster as they tapped on the door, there was no response but heard loud movements and voices within. They peeped in and to their surprise they saw women sitting naked without a single piece of cloth on their bodies. On seeing them peeping inside they sat down and said, "This is our condition, how can we come out to vote? Be generous to give your sarees and we promise to cast our votes in your favour". Tears came in the eyes of Priti and Sarla as they realized that they could not have given their sarees and helped them.The fact that the women in the villages were so poor came as a shock to them. They then moved on to the ladies of well to do families. They were dressed up so well that no part of the body could be seen. They even covered their faces and looked through their veils only. They moved fast to attend to their homely duties. They did not even know where their front door was. They were kept absolutely ignorant about everything. They toiled day in and day out fully covering their faces attending happily to their odd jobs of cooking and looking after the children and the ailing and the old. All this took Priti and Sarla by surprise.

They then moved on to Karuna. Sarla had a very good voice. She also knew well the dialect of this area. So she came down the truck, took the mike in her hand and sang in her sweet voice. It was as if a nightingale called out to all in her eloquent voice to gather there. All became curious and ran towards the truck. Her eloquent voice that vibrated in the air made the morning so pleasant. Priti took advantage of it and started to deliver her message,

"Brothers and sisters, we are a free nation and need to live effectively, enjoyably and successfully. Like the moon we need to come out of the clouds and shine brightly".

Sarla quietly pinched Priti and said in her ear softly,

"They do not understand your flowery speech".

Priti then changed and continued,

"What I mean to say is that we should get our basic rights, to live happily. Remember you get all these if you vote for the right person. So vote for the Professor as he stands to represent you and all that you need".

Sarla was there to help Priti for sometime, but she went off as her classes had started.

On returning home Sarla told Amma,
"The days of canvassing are almost coming to an end. They have entered their last phase. Mama has so far failed to make his appearance on the stage. He has been false to all his promises. Baba feels that his presence with them in the public would make a big difference. They are attracting huge crowds, but such crowds require a solid backing of the party leader at least once".
Poor Amma felt absolutely helpless. She tried again to contact her dear brother but the answer was the same, "At the moment the leader is too busy. He will consider it when he gets time".
Amma was highly depressed as she could see that her move that she took to convince all was falling back upon her. But it was too late. The leap has already been taken and there was no going back. Facing the travails and uncertainties, doubts began to rise whether it was wise to believe in the words of a politician. Even Priti was pretty sure, after Mama's disappearance, that she was losing a battle which she has fought with courage, conviction and to the best of her abilities.

Bhaiya and Sarla moved out from the scene as bhaya was needed at home and Sarla's classes had begun. Priti felt lonely and was slightly disturbed. Bhaiya understood worldly situations very well but Baba was a saint. For him life was holy and sacred. There should not be bad thoughts and bad deeds. One needs to walk the path of life with joy and happiness. When Baba asked

Priti to address people, she spoke to the audience. All types and all classes of people were there. Old and young, men and women heard her in rapt attention wondering at her capabilities. In this village in which they landed four boys came out and told Baba, "Next is our village, please come there and we can assure you of the support of our village". Priti could see that their eyes were on her, so she insisted that Baba should not go there. But Baba saw no harm and asked the driver to turn in that direction.Thiree boys got a good crowd and asked Priti to address it. She could well see their design, so she refused saying that she was tired and not in a mood to speak. Baba then stood up to speak. The boys were disappointed. Baba spoke about his party, about himself, and of how he could change the very colour of the village if voted to power. The enthusiastic crowd clapped loudly and assured of its support. Baba was happy. It became dark by this time so the boys offered their place for rest. Baba would agree to everything. Priti had a terrible time as they took her inside to rest with the ladies. Sisters and mothers soon disappeared and one can well understand the plight of poor Priti. While one offered her a drink so that she could relax, the other sat too close to her to talk, another tried to take her hand while the fourth smiled and addressed her 'my sweet queen'. Things were going from bad to worse, when Priti in a clever way got up and said "I have to go and get my night dress which Baba has". Quickly she ran out towards Baba's room and lay by the side of her father.

"I knew you will not be comfortable without me" Baba said innocently.

"Yes Baba I have got into a bad habit of not getting sleep without lying down by your side. So I have come running to you. Also I did not have my night suit to change into". Priti spoke loudly the latter portion to convince those ruffians. She then asked the boys to go out for she must change. They were disappointed and had to leave. Priti hurriedly bolted the door from inside. The boys stood waiting for her for sometime and had to leave in despair. Priti took a deep breath of relief as she lay by the side of her Baba. She cried bitterly and cursed her mother who found in her a convenient tool to solve all her problems, never ever giving a slightest thought to her feelings and to her safety.

When they entered the next village, they were quite surprised that the sarpanch of the village greeted them and requested them to come over and have lunch with them, a favour they never got anywhere. Was it because Baba was the winning candidate, they wondered. After taking lunch they sat down and had a good chat. Sarpanch began by asking the Professor,
"You look to be quite simple, coming from a profession well known for its honesty and dignity. How is it that you have entered this arena of cunning and deceit?"
"I came into this field on the insistence of my wife. She happens to have a brother doing very well in this field. He is the well known leader of the K.M.P party, Mr. Shibban Lal Saxena", Professor replied proudly.
"I believe he was intelligent enough to see that he could easily fool you, perhaps to get some advantage for himself", said sarpanch taking a dig at the politician.
"But I have been attracting large crowds in whichever

village I went. I found a good applause from them also. Our speeches have convinced them to vote for me. I am pretty sure that I will succeed in my mission", replied Professor with a feeling of elation.

"Do you think that the crowd that gathered round you has any meaning?" asked the sarpanch.

"But they are the ones that must decide and cast their votes accordingly" Professor replied.

"They have little or no intelligence. The set up of each village is such, that it is put under the guidance of a surpanch. The people of that village regard him as their leader and need to go about only under his orders. They are like the herd which must follow the one who takes them out in different directions. They know well that they would go astray, if they do not follow their master's directions. If they come out in large numbers and applaud you, it is to enjoy your music, they are happy to see in their village people coming from the city with their different culture and dress. And above all they are thrilled to see and hear your daughter speak to them", sarpanch explained to the Professor.

"Shiban Lal had promised to come, but he tells us that he is too busy these days" Professor said.

"A very good excuse to make after putting you into all this trouble. This very well shows what a fool he has made of you. Professor ji, no one in the field of politics saves us but ourselves. No one can and no one may. We must ourselves walk the path", explained sarpanch. Baba was taken aback, as he now understood the entire game. Frustration overtook him as the nagging self doubts rose high within him. He was absolutely quiet.

There was complete silence for some time which was broken by sarpanch,
"But I assure you that all the votes of this village will go for you as I want a man of my caste to be elected here. You are of my caste". Baba thanked sarpunch for his help and the good lunch that he had after a good long time. Then both Priti and Baba left. He refused to give any more speeches. Baba wanted to go back but this option he had given up long back. He was miserable. Who was he to blame? His wife, himself or Shibban? He did not know. But the only alternative before him was to continue, in any way either disheartened or with a firm mind. He was highly agitated. But still there was the last hope left, the appearance of Shibban on the stage. A desperate call was given by Priti to her Amma.
"Amma we took mamaji's words too seriously. We believed in him and he has made a fool of us. You can make a last effort to call him up and request him to make his appearance and help us".
Accordingly Amma tried again but once again she had the same fate. This time it was worse as no one in the office even cared to answer her back.

According to the rules, the campaigning had to stop and the day of voting came. Baba appointed some of his men at the few polling booths to watch the reaction of the people whom he had addressed day in and day out. What came out was what the sarpanch had told him.

"Not one vote was cast in your favour except in the village where the sarpanch himself stood at the gate of the booth". This was what was conveyed to him by those appointed by him. But he refused to believe them. He felt that his labour and hard work would not go waste like that. He waited eagerly and anxiously for the results to be announced formally. Hopes still lingering told Baba that he was sure to be chosen. Finally the results were announced that the rival candidate had defeated him with a heavy margin. No more guessing, no more dreams and no more hopes, all these were broken and shattered in no time. A severe gloom surrounded the family. No one could blame anyone as each member had contributed towards the fatal decision. Baba had spent all his money on this great venture which he got after retirement. But they say that hopes never die so they all believed that as Baba's performance was pretty good at least he will get back his security deposit money, which was also a considerable amount and the family would have something to fall back upon. But the bolt from the blue fell when they got the news that Baba had lost his security deposit as he could not even muster up the number of votes required for it.

Baba had no one close to him, a friend, a colleague, a relation, a senior in whom he could have placed his faith, to tell him that such a step would bring bad luck and ruin his family. As he was the only earning member, he should have well desisted from a step that was likely to bring calamity which he would regret through out his life. Poor Baba, with no knowledge and acumen of a politician, merely on the insistence of his wife, jumped into an arena never known to him before. He jumped with full vigour never doubting that he might fall flat.

Looking forward and aspiring for better days ahead to come, the family landed in utter darkness and desperation. It was very difficult for them to accept their error so they laid the entire blame on Shibban and had some consolation. But whoever was to be blamed they saw before them dismal days ahead. Poor Amma, simple as she was, failed to make the distinction between her own world and that of a politician. The world of the politician is for those who are clever and who have nothing to stake except their own selves. Her case was entirely different. She carried the responsibility of so many. All in the family were dependent on her decisions. But if doubts arose they were soon pooh poohed by her dear brother. A dreary night awaited them, the bright light of the day was over. Amma was speechless as she was highly agitated within. She saw clearly what lay before her. She had watered her dreams with optimism, but now only fear and worry remained. The blow was too severe and the pain it caused was to remain for ever in her life. She was badly shaken as she looked to the days ahead. Thorns lay on her path that she must tread now. She lost all hopes for better days. Her silence worried all as it was more eloquent than her words. For her the life she had passed with ease and comfort was over. Her life was to her an arduous road too difficult to traverse. It was as if she had fallen asleep and was seeing a beautiful dream which soon turned into a nightmare that woke her up with a dread of what would happen next. How was she to marry her six daughters? But, poor thing, she was so bewildered she did not know how to react to the situation. Cry? Would she gain anything? Laugh? That was not possible. The answer lay in moving ahead quietly accepting the situation.

Baba gathered his strength because of his faith in God. He had confidence in his ability and in his honesty. He kept his head high and greeted all with a smile. He had retired recently to take rest after a long spell of hard work and lead an easy life. Instead he walked out in search of a job to meet the needs of the family. With no grudges, with no regrets, and with no complaints he worked harder than ever to lift the family from the gloom of loss and despair.

After some time to the surprise of all, one day Shibban entered this home, thumping as usual his foot on the stairs. He was surprised that no one came to greet him. Where were the six children he wondered and looked here and there. They all had hidden themselves and no one came forward even to offer him a seat. Priti ran to inform her Amma that Mama had finally arrived. Shibban Ji stood in the hall for sometime a little amazed and then drew the chair from the balcony and sat down. The infuriated sister entered the hall, drew a chair and sat beside the brother in silence. Shibban broke the silence,

"You know sister I could not get time to visit the constituency of your husband as I was too busy".

"But what about your tall promises that you made and the assurances that you gave"? asked Amma much annoyed.

"Professor must have got good knowledge of the political world. I am sure next time if he stands after five years he will be definitely elected. Is the lunch ready?" said Shibban.

Amma lost the balance and the cool of her mind and answered him back,

"You did not have the time for us, how can we have the time to worry about you. There is no food left for you in our kitchen. Do not try to make a fool of innocent people like us. We have understood you very well. If you have any shame left you will not make your appearance here again".

Insulted and humiliated, Shibban sat quietly for a few minutes and then slowly got up, walked down the stairs and hurriedly left the house.

The two followers waiting downstairs followed him wondering why the lunch did not come to them.

□

Specs, Umbrella and Watch

Mamta was a young girl, beautiful, full of energy and enthusiasm with many dreams in her eyes. But the kind of existence she had, never allowed her to express herself. She was a soft spoken and a sweet girl who gave respect and attention to all her elders with sincerity. Humility and tolerance characterized her behaviour. She wanted to study, but with poor means of her parents she could not fulfil her desire. She was denied opportunities and could never get what she looked for her self.

She became fourteen, a difficult time for the parents to carry on their responsibilities. They married her off to a rich business man, doing well in his own business and making good money. He was double her age, his first wife had expired and had left a son of almost Mamta's age. The man was earning well and that was his great asset, which overshadowed all his defects. He was not good looking, uneducated and slightly fat. But it did not matter. He stood a good chance in the marriage market. Many were ready to come to him, but Mamta was lucky to be his choice. This was a common occurrence in the society where the parents could not afford to offer a handsome dowry. Mamta had no choice in this selection and the wish of the elders found its way.

She had to be satisfied and had to bend down before her adversaries because they were more powerful than herself.

She became a good and a dutiful wife. But the husband was too possessive and did not allow his very young and very beautiful wife to go outside and mix with the neighbours and others fearing the trouble that he may land in. When he went out, he locked the door from outside. She could see the outside world and rush of the city from the window of her room which was on the first floor. Amongst others she saw on the road young girls of her age rushing to their schools in the morning. She loved to see them returning home in the afternoon, tired yet happy. She envied them wishing her self to be one of them.

Her husband was rich and had a lot of money, so she thought that he could easily send her to school. So one day picking up courage she said to her husband,
"You see I always wanted to study but my parents were poor. You have a lot of money so you can easily send me to school".
Ram was annoyed but suppressing his anger he said, "You will feel ashamed sitting with children who are five years old as you do not know even a,b,c. The best is to study at home and then think of all this".
"But who will teach me at home?" she waited for an answer, but getting no reply she said, "Can you teach me?"
Ram tried to control his temper as he felt irritated and insulted. He spoke softly, "Look here, my dear, they are studying so that they can get a good, rich husband.

But luckily you already have got one, so there is no need to waste your energy".

Poor Mamta, unhappy and unsatisfied, had to accept her fate quietly. She lived as a good, obedient and dutiful wife, looking after household jobs and giving birth to one daughter and two sons. As she was too immature to carry on her slender soulders the heavy burden of looking after her small children and her household jobs, Ram went to Mamta's village and spoke to her father, "Dada, if you allow me I can take your son, Ashok with me. I am usually on business tours outside the city and Mamta feels very nervous when left alone. Her small brother will give her good company and I will take good care of him." The poor father agreed but the mother replied, "All girls feel that way but gradually she will get adjusted." She felt too uneasy in parting with her son.

"No Mai, I will give him good education, which is not possible here in this small village. He will get a good job and get a good place in society", said Ram. This temptation was too difficult to resist and both readily gave Ashok the permission to go, to join his sister and to look for a better life.

Ashok proved to be a great asset. When free from school and studies, he was ready to help his sister. He would look after the children, play with them and was a good and a loving companion to his dear sister when the husband was out on business tours. At times he went to the market for purchasing some odd things. The son Prahalad, from the first wife was almost of Mamta's age. Ram himself took care of him, keeping him always away from his new bride and always by his side. He took his food with his father, and when moving out he was always with him. He initiated him into the business. He knew only the company of his father. He was not interested either in his new mother or small sister and brothers. His father was his only concern.

Ashok, Mamta's brother, would take her sister's little son, ten months old, for an outing in the morning and evening when she was busy cooking. He was very cute, healthy, bubbling with energy and life, an exact replica of his pretty mother, clapping with his tiny hands, smiling while enjoying the stroll, sitting on the shoulders of his Mama. Often getting tired, Ashok would make him sit on the Professor's verandah and allow him to play there. The professor had six daughters all studying and doing well in their studies. They moved together and had a lot of fun. At times, moving out, they would watch this little child and were tempted to play with him. Once Kamla asked,

"Whose child is this?"

"Ram Bhardwaj, the business man, who lives two houses away in your line" replied Ashok.

Ashok would go home and talk about these sisters at Professor's house and how they played with the child and often picked him up and the child would touch their cheeks and make a loud noise in sheer joy. Mamta had often seen these sisters going to and returning from their school, college and university. She longed to be one of them. But as luck would have it, here she was with three children, an aged husband, over possessive, never allowing her to meet even the ladies and girls of the neighborhood. One day as Sarla played with the child, Ashok told her that his sister, the child's mother would like to come and meet them. Sarla most readily said, "She is most welcome any time in the afternoon". Ashok conveyed the message to his sister. Mamta had to take the permission of her husband. It was a difficult task but it was she who had to act. No one would do it for her. She had to walk the path. So the day when the husband had returned after a long tour and had his dinner Mamta went to his bed a little early. She saw him in a very good mood. So with unflinching determination, she turned towards him that night and took the courage to say,

"You know dear, a little ahead is the house of a Professer, where there are only girls. I sometimes feel so lonely when you are away on long tours. If you allow I can go and sit with them and learn some valuable things in their good company. They can teach me knitting, sewing, and also give me some knowledge of a, b, c."

Ram said "But you have to be careful that as long as I am here you will not move out".

"O, for sure as long as I have your company why should I think of going to them? Sometimes as I watch them from the window, I envy them and pity myself", sighed Mamta.

"What? you are not satisfied with me?" asked Ram, highly annoyed. Sensing trouble Mamta spoke sweetly, "I am very happy with you. It is my luck that has brought me to you". Ram cooled down and Mamta continued, "All that I ask for is that once in a while for a little change I can go there".

The husband thought for some time and then said, "Make sure that you do not move out to the next house and then to the next".

"It is my promise that I shall act according to your order", replied Mamta showing great concern.

With great difficulty and after too many heart breaks Mamta succeeded in getting his permission to go twice a week and that too for two hours a day.

"You know" said Mamta making a serious face "I cannot be absent from the house longer than that as so much work has to be done. I can assure you that I will keep up to my promise. You need to know well that I hate to neglect my household duties and my responsibilities to all the members here at home".

Mamta used all her means and words at her command to get his permission. The wise man doubted but caught in a tricky situation agreed to what his wife wanted. At last Mamta succeeded, and in sheer joy she closed her eyes and promised Hanuman Ji ladoos next Tuesday. It was a herculean task for Mamta as Ram always felt that if he gave freedom to his wife, he was sure to land into trouble. Mamta's life had become like a ship caught in a heavy storm. But she never lost hope and was sure that some day she would reach a situation that would be to her heart's content. Underlying this optimism she had the confidence that her situation was only temporary.

Everyday on getting up she would ask her brother, "Is your brother-in-law going on tour to day?"

"Not that I know of", was Ashok's usual reply.

Getting impatient she asked her husband one day, "You have not gone on a tour for a long time?"

"Are you sick of me?" enquired Ram getting highly agitated.

"Not at all, I asked because every Tuesday you definitely

go on your tour" explained Mamta politely.
"Don't worry, I will be here this whole month and move out only after that", replied Ram.
Mamta's heart sank but with a sweet smile she said,
"Oh! that will be wonderful".
She waited impatiently for the time to pass, only her impatience was making it too long. At last the day arrived and he came to tell his wife,
"I will be back after a fortnight".
"O, that will be too long and I hate it. But the business is also very important", replied Mamta with all seriousness.
"Yes dear" said Ram and went off.

Her plans were ready. She was on her way to the Professor's house, escorted by her young brother. Soon they reached the house and Ashok introduced her sister to the family. Courteous and polite, Kamla offered her a seat and they had a nice chat together. She enjoyed being with them and told them that she envied the sisters as she saw them going to school. But her fate was only to sit at the window and look at them. Unsatisfied longings and unfulfilled desires made her sad. Soon she became a constant visitor and was happy with the family. She started learning knitting and stitching. When Ram would return, she would show him her achievements.

Day in and day out if she had to talk, it was only about the six sisters.
"They are so good. Each sister has a unique quality. If one is good in music, the other excels in dance, still other in knitting and all are too good in their studies".

"Are they helpful and do they give you any attention as you are senior to them all", asked Ram.
"They are very courteous to me and very helpful and that is why I have learnt so much. I will move on with them............", said Mamta.
Ram would nod as she incessantly talked about the six sisters. She had no other topic to talk about, not even the children or any household event. He often got bored but allowed her to go on.

One night, she came to Ram, who was not in a good mood because of some loss in business. Without sensing his mood, as usual she started harping on her favourite subject, the six sisters. Ram lost his temper and gave her a slap on her cheek and said much annoyed,
"I am tired of hearing all your nonsense. You have no other topic than the six sisters. You are neither bothered about the children nor about me".
Big tears rolled down the cheeks of Mamta for the slap was too harsh for her soft tender cheeks. Crying, she left his bed and ran out of the room and came to the children's room and slept with them. In the morning when she looked into the mirror she saw her swollen face which was hurting her badly. But at the same time she also realized her mistake. She took an oath that henceforth she would be careful and not talk about the six sisters who gave her good company and all her thoughts were about them only.

She waited for her husband to go on his business tour. After he left, she finished her household jobs and quickly moved towards her destination, the house of the six sisters. She had seen Priti, the eldest amongst the six sisters, helping out many students in the subject of English. It was a subject in which the Indian students are usually weak. Even a boy was coming from a distance seeking her help. She never refused any one for the father had told her "the highest form of charity is to help one to get on well in studies". Priti was one who would go out of her way, even to her inconvenience, if it came to help others to learn. Mamta admired her and felt that she was a perfect girl, her ideal. Every thing about her was so good, the way she walked with a lovely gait, the way she dressed, the way she put her specs and her watch on her left hand, and while moving out the umbrella which she always carried, she opened to save herself from the sun and the rains. She yearned to be like her.

One day when Priti was alone, busy writing something, Mamta entered her room and sat there quietly for sometime waiting for her to finish. Priti asked her when she looked up,

"You have come after a good long time?"

"Yes I was waiting for my husband to go and this time he took a long time to go", replied Mamta.

"Don't you feel lonely without him?" asked Priti casually as she had nothing else to talk about.

"Not at all", Mamta emphasised.

Priti looked at her quite surprised.

Mamta tried to speak coolly, "Because the children are there".

Priti smiled back.

"You know I have one great desire". Mamta stopped as Priti looked at her to continue and when she did not, she asked, "What desire is that?" But Mamta remained

quiet trying hard to say something.
"I hope I am not too inquisitive?" said Priti.
"You know Priti you are my ideal and it is my desire to be just like you. I admire you", Mamta answered.
Priti blushed and asked "What is in me that appeals to you?"
"I want to put on specs, put a watch on my left hand wrist, hold an umbrella and then walk slowly and steadily like you", replied Mamta.
Priti had a hearty laugh and holding herself with difficulty, she said, "You can very well do all this, there is no problem".
"There is a serious problem" spoke Mamta in a reflective mood. "All these things go well only because you are so learned".
"Learned? How?" Priti was quite surprised.
"You have done your B.A. in the college, pursuing your studies you have completed M.A in the university. You are still on the move to do your research work. I am an illiterate person with not even the knowledge of a,b.c".

Priti stopped laughing as Mamta continued, "I always wanted to go to school and study. My parents were very poor. I was unlucky and unfortunate to be beautiful and to become fifteen. Soon my parents married me, happy to get rid of their responsibilities, despite my refusal. I accepted my fate, hoping that what was denied to me in my village, I will get in the city. But the man I got was only interested in satisfying his desires, whims and fancies. He got furious when I mentioned what I wanted. I had no way out, but to accept my fate. I suppressed my feelings but coming in contact with you all, those feelings have roused again within me. I just request you to teach me English, as Hindi I will manage myself. If then I hold an umbrella, wear a watch on my left hand and wear specs, it will give a meaning and a look that will be really fascinating, which I find in you".

Priti heard Mamta's long story with patience and remarked,

"Well Didi, I never refuse any one to offer my help especially when it comes to studies. So I cannot say no to you also, but at the moment I am very busy writing my thesis, I can only afford to give you very little time, which may not be really helpful to you".

"No problem, your little time will be a great boon for me. I have heard a lot about your wonderful ways of teaching".

Poor Priti, caught in the trap could only smile back.

"So one day I will put on specs, wear watch on my wrist and hold an umbrella and then walk slowly and steadily! I see my dreams coming true!!" Mamta exclaimed in sheer joy.

Much amused Priti could only say, "Let us try".

First with folded hands and then trying to touch Priti's feet she bent down to express her thankfulness. Priti held her and said,

"Please don't do all that. I just want to see you happy and if I can do something towards it, I will consider myself lucky. You know, to get happiness is to make others happy".

So they both started on their journey together with enthusiasm and earnestness. Mamta still being young and desirous to learn made a hard and sincere effort and succeeded well. Priti was surprised that she picked up fast. Mamta devoted all her time that she got when she was free from her household jobs to her studies only. An effort succeeds where there is joy in doing it. So Priti taught and Mamta learnt both doing their best moved fast ahead.

Ram was happy that his wife no longer talked about those "blessed six sisters" any more. He never had an inkling how she was moving fast with them without his knowledge.

One day he saw her doing puja, so he asked Mamta, "Why all of a sudden you have become so serious and started all this nonsense?"
"You know that lady that comes here sometimes to give Prasad?"
Ram nodded. Mamta continued, "It is she who told me that it does good to the family for it works towards the happiness and welfare of all its members. It also creates positivity in the mind of the individual who performs the puja and brings a lot of confidence. With all this it makes her competent to make the life of the family better". She repeated only Priti's words but dare not tell her name. The six sisters had now become her ideal. But she had become clever. She knew well that there were only two ways of meeting difficulties. You alter the difficulty, which she could not, so she altered herself to meet them. She never spoke about the six sisters and showed that she was not interested in them. Ram was quite satisfied yet surprised. He kept quiet for a good long time but could not resist long and asked Mamta "What are the lessons that you are learning these days from your great teachers, the great six sisters?"
"I hardly go to them as I find little time from my

household work. Then the children also need some attention. Attending to all this I get very tired so I lie down and take rest", replied Mamta in a disinterested way.

Ram noticed that when she went to the sisters, she looked so bright and happy, but on his return from the tour this time she looked so dull and gloomy. Always she was attending to her household jobs, but never so disgusted as at the moment. Ram thought for some time and then said,

"Your going to the sisters was a good change for you. You need to spend some good time with them when I am away. They can also help you to learn how to read and write, enough to go through the addresses when the post man arrives, put your signatures when required or to be able to read the messages that I some time send".

Overjoyed, her face lighted up, but hiding all her feelings she said,

"They are all too busy with their studies, I wonder if they can help me. But I can take a chance and request them and tell them that it is your wish that I must learn something. They hold you in high esteem, I am sure that they will comply".

Mamta was clever to speak in a way that her husband wanted her to speak, well hiding the fact that the process had already begun and these six Sisters fully controlled her mind and heart and she loved to imitate them in all their ways. Ram was quite satisfied. "We had a good long time talking to each other. Children have gone off to sleep so let us also lie down", said Ram. Mamta quietly obeyed.

Time rolled on. The six sisters got an interesting Didi, with her strange and unusual thoughts and amusing ways. Mamta DiDi in return brightened her otherwise dull life which she had to spend in doing only household jobs, looking after her children and obeying the orders of her old husband. Priti advised Mamta one day,

"Now that you have learnt so much, you can appear for eighth class government examination, passing which you can get a certificate, which can help you greatly in your later life".

A great idea but the problem was how to obtain the husband's permission, without which she could not proceed an inch. The thought occupied her mind and she got busy how to go about it. The husband, she knew well was against it. He never gave much value to education for married women. Even then Mamta finding a good opportunity told her husband:

"If you permit me I can appear and get a government certificate for all that I have learnt so far. It would be so good".

But Ram replied,

"You do not need certificates to be a good wife. I do not have any certificate, yet I am a successful business man, earning a good amount of money".

Ram was highly annoyed with Mamta. She saw her dreams crashing down. She made a number of efforts, but failed. It was not possible to sit for the examination secretly. Yet full of life and energy, she was unwilling to accept defeat. Optimistic in her outlook she argued within herself that the dark night of disappointment has to be a temporary state and must pass off. Difficulties do crop up but they need to be met with courage. Like the dark night these human difficulties also pass off.

These are bound to disappear only if she did not give up making efforts towards what she wanted to be. Something good had to emerge and it would be foolish on her part to lose patience or hopes. She refused to be a victim of frustration. She tried to focus on this bent of mind rather than the difficulty she was facing. She was brave and courageous, strong enough to take another leap.

Luckily or unluckily Ram on a return from his business tour fell seriously ill. Mamta took great care of him and never left his side, giving him all support. She prayed to God to give him a speedy recovery. Ram was very much touched by her loving concern. She could read the prescription given by the doctor and give him the right medicine and at the right time and in the right manner. The doctor also wrote how and what diet he required. Mamta carefully read it and followed it religiously. Ram took a long time to restore his energies to get out of his bed. He realised well that it was all due to the loving care of his wife.

Mamta felt that it was the right time for her to ask for a favour. She stood a good chance to get his permission for what she wanted. She had lovingly sponged his body and was helping him to lie down when she spoke sweetly,

"My dear, give this idea a thought that if I get a certificate for all the little I have learnt, it will give me a boost and will make me so happy".

In a good mood, what he had denied so many times to Mamta, he readily accepted and said,

"There is no harm in achieving something that makes you happy".

"I have to sit with girl- students only. It is only one hour daily for a week", Mamta informed Ram.

Ram knew well that she was following Priti's dictum as against his own wishes. But he was much impressed by the loving care and attention that she gave to him during his serious and long illness. He was willing to be a part of her happiness so he readily accepted what did not really matter to him, but gave her what she wanted and made her happy. While giving Ram his medicine she burst out in sheer joy,

"You are so good, so caring and so loving. I thank you so much for every thing".

Ram only smiled back. Soon he got out of his bed and was busy with his work.

After getting the permission to sit in the examination Mamta could now move on towards her destination without disturbances. Hiding and secrecy, she knew well, would not work for all times and in all situations. She felt relaxed and started working very hard day in and day out, when the husband was away and a little with care when he was with her. The dates were announced and finally the day came. She went to the examination hall without fear and in full peace. It was a great experience to sit in the public with others. Not bothered, not even nervous, she answered her question papers with full concentration. Hard work never goes unrewarded. To the surprise of all, she not only passed out but could get a good second division. Though it meant nothing to the husband, it was a great achievement for Mamta. The six sisters were profuse in giving their praises and warmly congratulated her. They were happy also because their efforts had not gone waste.

One step opened before Mamta, the possibility of another leap that she could now take to realize her dream. Life showed Mamta hundred reasons to cry, but a courageous spirit that she was she showed life that she had a thousand reasons to smile. The life that otherwise would have been a drag became a fragrance. Had she allowed herself to remain in the dilemma of inaction she would have never arrived at this goal. Her optimism gave her confidence and she walked on a difficult path never wavering or intending to give up. Anxieties did come on her way to an uphill task but she continued to climb undauntedly. Life was never a bed of roses for her but what was important for her was that she never gave up hopes.

Priti's next move was to advise Mamta to work hard for high school examination. It was an achievement, something that was considered quite meaningful in life. Priti's advice to Mamta was an order for her from the heavens and needed to be complied with at any cost what so ever. Mamta smiled back and said to Priti,
"But you will be there with me for no battle can be fought alone".
Priti admired Mamta's undaunted courage, shook hands with her and said, "By all means I will always be there by your side". It was a signal for Mamta that another battle was there before her and she must fight bravely and must conquer it. She took a pledge, "From today only I will work hard and do my very best". Priti

encouraged her with a nod and her pretty smile. Mamta came back home, the idea given by Priti possessed her and soon it became a passion with her.

Her only thought was that of studies, to get a high school certificate and for that she would leave no stone unturned. She quietly got books from the market and started her work. With a guide like Priti she was ready for the most difficult battle.

The sisters were too busy preparing for their exams and Priti in giving final touches to her thesis. So no one was in a mood to give any company to Mamta. She therefore stayed back at home, never moving out to the Professor's house. It was a surprise to all. She was quietly utilising time to learn all that Priti had taught. Mamta had stopped going to the Professor's house and it was brought to the notice of Ram, who asked one day, "Dear, I hear that you have stopped going to the house of the six sisters. It is hard to believe. What has happened? Have you quarrelled with them?"

"Oh no, they are such good souls that they will never quarrel with any one, least of all with me. It is just that I give more time to my children that I find it very difficult to go to them. You know they are fast growing up and need my attention. I also help them in their studies".

"I am quite surprised that you never even mention them in your talks. How is your dear Priti?" asked Ram making faces for he hated her. He was taken aback because the most pressing problem would not keep her away from her visits to the sisters.

"Why? She must be all right". Replied Mamta unconcerned.

"Their company you so much liked. You learnt so much from them. They occupied your mind and heart and for no reason you have left them. It greatly puzzles me", said Ram watching closely Mamta's reaction.

"If you say I can start my visits" said Mamta showing that she was least interested in this topic.

"It's your wish", said Ram and was out on his business tour.

Mamta had a hearty laugh behind Ram's back. She had learnt well how to speak before her husband and the way he wanted.

Time rolled on. Three years passed. All were busy in their own affairs. Mamta as usual was busy with her household works, devoting all the remaining time that she had to her studies. She studied day in and day out as permitted by her odd circumstances. Priti worked hard to teach English in her best way. It is a subject quite difficult for Indian students to grasp. They do well in other subjects, but get pulled down when it comes to English language. Priti's concentrated efforts brought Mamta to a point of confidence and she sat for her High School Examination. She knew well that being a private candidate, despite her best efforts, she stood little chance of success, when she would be marked with the regular students.

Mamta's aspirations were too high but to the surprise of all the impossible became possible. Here she was standing amongst the best successful candidates of High School examination. She had touched the heights. She was so happy because she could well be counted amongst the educated, a literate lady. She could now walk like Priti holding an umbrella, putting on specs and having a watch on her wrist. She was overjoyed that she had realized her dream. She wanted to give Priti a surprise.

She went to the market and bought specs, a red umbrella and a small pretty watch. She tied the watch on her left wrist, put the specs on and opened her bright umbrella and trying to walk with Priti's gait she reached the Professor's house. She stopped and stood in the verandah. She called Priti loudly and asked her to come down soon. Priti ran down the stairs with great speed. She was quite amused at what she saw before her. Lo! Didi was there in her unusual style standing before her with a pretty watch on her wrist holding an open colourful umbrella, sweetly smiling and coming towards Priti with a slow gait. Priti admiring her, saluted her. She then said,
"My heartiest congratulations to you on your great achievement! Your dream has come true!"
Mamta bowed down with love and said, "It is you who has made all this possible".
"Not at all. It is your undaunted courage and consistent efforts that have made you what you are and I salute you", Priti replied saluting her again.

Priti sank into Mamta's heart and soul and was always present there. A good time elapsed and Priti got married to an army officer and moved out of Lucknow to distant places in the south. She lost contact with Mamta, one who was by her side almost every day. But by a strange turn of events, she was present by Mamta's bed side during the last moments of her life. The nurse had dressed her up in spotless white. Beautiful as she was she looked like an angel, calm and quiet. She neither spoke, nor ever opened her eyes. She lay life-less in a state of semi- consciousness. But when Priti called out\"Didda", for that was how she addressed her, Mamta's body quivered and to the surprise of the nurse and all those who stood there, she tried hard to make some movement. She recognized well the voice of Priti, one who was a part of her soul. Slowly and softly she opened her eyes, and smiling looked into the eyes of Priti trying hard to tell her what all had passed with her when she was away from her. She lifted her weak hand and lovingly held Priti's, but all that she could utter to someone standing by was "Can't you see my Priti has come, go and get some sweets for her". After that she loosened her hold of Priti's hand and let it go. She then slowly and softly closed her eyes, never to open them again.

Tears rolled down Priti's cheeks on hearing that Mamta had gone for ever. She closed her eyes and prayed to God, "O Lord, give her peace. But do allow such undaunted brave souls to come into this world again and again".

My God

The professor would sit every evening with his six daughters to tell them about the principles, if followed would make their lives happy. Things were not clear to the children, so Priti asked one day:
"Baba you say that we must always love and remember God. But how are we to love and remember one whom we cannot see".
"But once you love Him dearly you will begin to see Him", replied Baba.
The six children were puzzled and were silent. But Priti in her silence thought hard over what Baba had told her. She being the eldest thought hard and understood things better than the rest. She got fixed up with ideas instilled in her little mind. These continued to hold her mind strongly and her love of God became stronger with every passing year as she grew up.

Priti had learnt to love God with all her heart and soul. Her life as she moved on became a real struggle and a great challenge for her. At times she was disgusted and disappointed as misfortunes after misfortunes followed. But the lesson she had learnt from her father gave her great strength. It made her to accept things with a smile. She moved forward, facing all, courageously determined that none could pull her down. She held her head high and walked forward willing to face all because of her intense faith in God.

Soon Baba left her. But the passion to visit temples and to hear the words of great men and teachers never left her. Whenever she got time for these, she never missed the opportunity. It was on one such visit to a temple of Rajasthan, she found someone who could illustrate clearly what her Baba had tried to explain.

It took Priti great labour and pain to reach the temple as the road leading to it was under construction and closed for the traffic. She somehow facing tremendous problems reached the temple as she was too keen to see it. On coming inside the temple, she went round bowing down to the numerous deities as she passed on and came to the main. All deities were dressed up in blue. But what surprised her was when she saw her Kanha dressed up in blue. She wondered why He was dressed up in blue. He ought to have been with His yellow 'pitambari'. She was puzzled. Her anxiety rose high so she looked around if anyone could help her. Those devotees that sat before the idol were in the same line as she was. She walked fast searching each and every corner of the temple for someone who could give an answer to her query. To her surprise, in one remote corner she saw a very old sadhu sitting with closed eyes in deep meditation. Priti sat down before him with folded hands. After ten minutes the sadhu slowly opened his eyes and looked up. He saw Priti and asked her,
"How can I help you, my child?"
"Why is Kanha in blue?" Priti asked humbly.

"To answer your query I have to narrate a long story of one very close to me and that will take a lot of time".

"It does not matter for I can sit for the whole evening and even for the whole night," Priti replied with great enthusiasm.

The sadhu thought for sometime and then started,

"My dear child there is a river that runs behind this temple, have you seen it?"

"Yes Baba I have seen it" replied Priti promptly.

"On the other side of the river" continued sadhu," there is a small village, I also happen to live there. In this village a gujjar lived with his small daughter, whom all the villagers called Gujjari. Her mother died at her birth and it was her father who brought her up. He happened to be a great devotee of Kanha so he brought his little daughter to this temple every day. Under the care and influence of her father she too became a devotee of Kanha. The father would tell her,

"You must love Kanha as you love me, because He is your well wisher".

"But Dada I love you because you love me and care for me. Also you are always with me and before me", Gujjari would innocently reply.

"He is also with you. Don't you see Him in the temple? He loves you, my dear child, only you have to love Him. I will get old and go away one day, but He will never leave you He will always be with you".

Gujjari's mind would be puzzled for sometime but she got relaxed when she started seeing her Kanha in this temple always smiling and calling her. With her simple small heart she started loving her Kanha who was for her personified in the idol of Kanha in this temple.

Under the care and influence of her father soon she grew up strong, tall and healthy, loving her Kanha and having sincere faith in Him. She danced with joy as she attended her father who was getting old and feeble. She looked after the cow, their only possession and she gave service to any one father would send her for.

The sadhu then stopped and gave his own interpretation of her:
"My dear child, the quality of life depends on our own relationships. The father had taught this lesson very well. The greatest gift this father could give to his daughter during all the ups and downs of life was Love. She had taught her to be content with what she had and rejoice in things as they were. The whole world belonged to her. In doing good to others she felt happy and that was her religion".The sadhu was then quiet for sometime, Priti wondered why? The sadhu then looked at Priti, took a long deep breath and began again.

"But to continue, as luck would have it, the father one evening got caught up in a storm which blew up all of a sudden while he was crossing the river. Because of his growing weakness, despite his best efforts, he was drowned and died. Gujjari cried bitterly day in and day out. She was too small, only eleven years old. She missed her father and did not know what to do when one night her father came in her dream and said,
"Now, my dear Gujjari, get up and stop crying. You are not alone. Have you forgotten your Kanha who is with you? He loves you so much. Hold his hand and move forward. I know you are a brave girl". She got up with a strong feeling that no more she was alone for Kanha

would take care of her. With faith in Him and confidence in her own self she started her life again.

She had nothing to fall back upon, only a small hut to give her shelter, a cow to give her sustenance, lessons that her father had taught her and her love for her Kanha. With great care she looked after her cow and took out milk early in the morning every day. The first thing she would do was to take a small jar of milk on her head and carry it to the temple. She would tie her 'ghangri' up so that it would not get wet and cross the river with a glowing face remembering that Kanha must be waiting for her eagerly. The pandits despised her as her offering stood nowhere before the offerings of the rich. But the owner's order that the offerings of the poorest had to be put before the idol made them grudgingly take the milk from Gujjari and put it before Kanha. They hastily and unwillingly obliged her. But Gujjari, whose entire concentration was on her Kanha, saw him eagerly drinking it. In fact he was waiting for it. When he finished he gave back a sweet smile of thanks to her. Gujjari would then smile back and sit for a while in the temple singing at times hymns in her sweet, melodious voice. She would then pick up her jar and return to wade through the waters and come back to her hut. She would then give a warm tender pat to the cow and enter the hut to rest.

Kanha of the temple was no idol for her but a reality. She loved him with all her mind and heart. Kanha did not remain confined to the temple but she saw him all round in all who were around her. All loved her. Loving and not expecting was the secret of her joy. She would be the first one to run and hold the hands of the blind and take him to the right direction. She could not see an old man carrying a heavy load on his head, bent and perspiring. She would gently take off his load and reach him to his destination. If any one needed help and was in trouble and wanted assistance, the one person who all remembered was this sweet small Gujjari. At any call of distress, she was the first to extend her helping hand. All loved her. The blossom of love made the air fragrant, the river murmured love along the valley and all including the beasts and the birds sang the song of love. Such was her life as she grew up alone with her Kanha protecting her.

For this sweet Gujjari a life without love was like a sunless garden where the flowers were dead. She was loving and was being loved by all and that brought warmth and richness to her life that perhaps nothing could bring. Love happened to her not because she tried hard for it, but because it came so naturally. If a mother came asking for some milk for her child who was crying for it, she would readily give her share of milk, without the thought ever disturbing her that she had to take her bread only with salt.

The sadhu then digressed and commented,
"My dear child, love is the ultimate truth that lies at the heart of creation and she had it in abundance without reading any of the philosophical books. She had no knowledge of the great Vedas or Upanishads. The path of Kanha is very difficult for the embodied souls to realize. But as Kanha himself says,
"I quickly come to those who offer me every action. Because they love me, I become their bondsman".

By cultivating the right attitude, she was spiritual and that was her meditation. She never focused on all that was wrong, that she was all alone in this vast world or she had only a hut as her possession and a cow to protect her and give her sustenance. Instead she focused on her love for Kanha. She never cribbed about what she did not have, but she spent time to remember her sweet Kanha, whose love gave her all and she took time to appreciate people around her and ran forward to help them with whatever little she had. There was no negativity in her life. Hers was the positive attitude and she rejoiced in her love of Kanha. The gist of all her worship was to be pure and to do good to others. She helped the needy because she saw Kanha there and never thought of any thing else, whether the person was old or young, of high caste or low caste or if he was rich or poor. In doing so she knew well that Kanha was pleased with her for she never saw him only as one present in the temple. She saw him every where in men and in nature. She danced with joy as life for her was so beautiful. She did not put her hand over her eyes and cried that it was all dark around. Instead she worked happily on the fields with farmers, did her odd household jobs and went about lending her helping hand to all those who needed her. She radiated light around her that brought a smile on every face as they watched her grow strong, healthy and so pretty.

Priti interrupted and asked with full reverence, "but Baba how do you know her so intimately, that you can describe her with such minute details?" The sadhu smiled and was quiet for some time. Then he raised his eyebrows and said,

"I was a small boy when she would often hold my hand and bring me to this temple. She instilled in me her love of Kanha. I was the one who was her admirer. It is because of her influence that you see me sitting here at this time in meditation. But as I look back, the years that I have spent under her care have been so precious for me, for I learnt the joy of loving and living. Life must be understood backwards but it needs to be lived forwards. That is what happened with me. I forget every thing when I begin to talk about her or even think of her. I can continue to talk about her incessantly and tell a lot about her but to cut it short I will just narrate one incident to put my point through that I have been talking about so far and also satisfy your curiosity about the blue dress that Kanha is putting on today.

Life continued with her in this way. Her daily visit to this temple, her satisfaction in helping out others, in being with her Kanha and offering him an early, first drink of her cow's milk were all a passion with her. It was raining hard for almost a week. The river had swollen up and small fishes had grown up in abundance. It was quite risky for her to wade through the waters in such a weather. But nothing could deter her from coming to this temple. On one such morning when the winds blew harder than ever and waves in the waters rose high Gujjari carefully tied her 'ghanghri' high up and slowly waded through the waters. Small fishes had grown up in abundance and were having a good time playing on the waves of the river. It so happened that a few small fishes jumped into her jar as the thin cloth covering the mouth of the jar was torn off due to harsh winds, of which she was absolutely unaware. Innocently as was her daily practice she came near the door of her Kanha's room and poured the milk out of her jar into the pandit's vessel. And lo! the fishes jumped out of the milk. Gujjari was taken aback and stood stunned. She thought for a while how such a thing could have happened. She had covered the jar with a thin old piece of cloth. Was it possible that it was torn off the jar due to strong winds, she wondered? Was it possible then that the rising waves of the waters had brought the fishes into her jar? She tried to analyze the situation as she stood absolutely dumb.

But you can now imagine the anger of the pandit standing there. Before Gujjari could speak, he threw the milk out of the room into the backyard, came up to Gujjari, caught hold of her hair, shook her head violently and gave two harsh slaps on her tender cheeks, shouting,
"This is what you do? You get fishes in your milk in this sacred temple of Krishna".
Not allowing her to speak and wanting to get rid of her forever the other pandit came forward and gave her two more slaps. The one holding her hair dragged her mercilessly out of the room and called for the darban and shouted,
"Turn her out of the temple and make sure that henceforth she never enters even the vicinity of this temple".
In a fit of anger the pandit did not allow her even her last glance at her dear Kanha.

Hurt badly and humiliated Gujjari walked out slowly towards the river and sat down for sometime by the side of the river. She put her hair in order, and pulling her 'ghanghri' up, she slowly waded through the waters of the river. She entered her hut and cried bitterly for being punished for no fault of hers. She did not take a morsel of bread or even a sip of milk. She lay down on her cot for the whole day, covering her face, and often sobbing loudly. She had not complained to any one though she was highly frustrated. It grew dark and the village was quiet, as all went off to sleep.

Gujjari also closed her door and put the latch on. She came to her cot and lay for sometime contemplating on what all had happened in the temple and that she had been punished for no fault of hers. At this time softly some one knocked at her door. She thought that someone who needed her assistance must have come for her. She got up for she must help if any one was in trouble. But today she was feeling weak, exhausted and a little disturbed. Reluctantly she opened the door. And lo! who stood before her. It was none but her Kanha from the temple. Gujjari, very angry, came in and sat down on her cot. Kanha closed the door and came in and sat on the cot before her. She turned her back towards Kanha in anger. Kanha got up and again sat facing her.

"But Gujjari why are you angry with me? What have I done?" Kanha said very sweetly.

"Yes I am very angry with you" replied Gujjari very much annoyed.

Kanha pleaded, "You know Gujjari holding on to anger is like holding on to a hot coal. You intend to throw it at me, but I can very well see that it is you who is getting burned".

Gujjari kept mum to show her anger.

Kanha sat watching her in silence for a few seconds.

"Have you taken your dinner?" Kanha broke the silence.

Gujjari maintained her quiet to show her anger.

"I am sure this anger must not have allowed you to take any thing" Kanha commented.

Again Gujjari maintained her silence to show how hurt she was.

"Dear Gujjari I have come running to you because I was sure that you must be hungry", said Kanha.

"What hungry? What running?" Gujjari at last broke her silence and in anger she said, "You witnessed everything, standing over there at your place, but never uttered a word when I was beaten, insulted and thrown out of the temple".

"You did not see the tears in my eyes, when I witnessed what was being done to you. Naturally you did not care to look at me as your imagination was out of focus", said Kanha.

"What? Out of focus?" she repeated in anger Kanha's words and continued, "You could have uttered a few words to that cruel pandit, you could have stopped them from ill treating me. But, no, you looked on to see me dragged out for no fault of mine. Those pandits hurt me so much and you tolerated it? Am I not justified in being angry with you?" shouted Gujjari with tears coming out of her eyes and flowing over her soft rosy cheeks that had gone red due to her anger.

"But, my sweet Gujjari, I am not allowed to speak in the temple", said Kanha.

"But you talk to me, Kanha",said Gujjari.

"That is through the eyes and heart and not through the mouth", replied Kanha.

"What?" Gujjari asked in surprise and in anger as she failed to understand what Kanha meant.

Poor Kanha, he stood puzzled. What was he to do? He folded his hands and said,

"Forgive me my sweet Gujjari, the only remedy for your anger is forgiveness. Do forgive me and calm your mind. I plead guilty, but you know even I have not taken a morsel since morning and finding the first opportunity I have come running to you".

On hearing this, that her Kanha had not taken anything since morning, Gujjari was pained and much disturbed. She took hold of Kanha's hands that were still clasped together begging for forgiveness and said,

"Come on we both have not taken anything, me in anger and you in repentance. Let us forget every thing as a bad dream". Gujjari smiled through her tears and got up to get the dinner. She got chapaties that she had cooked the previous day and milk in two wooden bowls. They sat down on the floor and enjoyed the simple dinner laughing and forgetting all that had happened in the temple.

"But Kanha there is a serious problem that I shall be facing", said Gujjari all of a sudden remembering something.

"And now what is that?" asked Kanha.

"How will I meet you? Those fat pandits will not allow me to come to the temple and bring you your share of milk. I shall feel so bad about it. If I do not see my Kanha in the morning, it will be very difficult for me to pass the day".

"You need not worry, for I will come here for you every day in the morning to take my share of milk from your hands or else make some arrangements", replied Kanha. "I cannot live with the thought that I cannot meet you whom I love and who loves me too" said Gujjari with a naughty smile.

"True, but I have already given you the solution. I will be here every morning", Kanha answered back.

"Sure, you promise, not to make any excuses later on, in which you are very clever", said Gujjari.

"When I promise I keep them", Kanha smiled back.

"I am helpless Kanha. But you are my life and how can I live without you?" entreated Gujjari.

Kanha kept on looking at her face, reflecting a heart full of love for him.

"Can I live without you, Gujjari?", asked Kanha lovingly, which very much satisfied her.

"Well Gujjari, we had a sumptuous dinner. It is getting late and I must return to the temple", said Kanha standing up to go. Gujjari got up to open the door. She saw it was raining hard. She turned round and holding Kanha's hand tight, said,

"I will not allow you to go in this bad whether. The river must be roaring. Its waves must rising high. My father died in a storm. I am sure you will be caught up by the hard blowing winds, rising waters and rains falling on your head. I lost my father once like that and now I cannot afford to lose you who is my only support".

"For me all this is nothing. I will safely reach the temple. You need not worry Gujjari" assured Kanha.

"I know you never care for yourself. But I do care for you. If you insist on going I will come with you" so saying she closed the door. Poor Kanha was helpless.

He becomes so when he faces those who surrender themselves completely to him.

Gujjari spread a worn out sheet on the foor and said, "You have to sleep here and go away early in the morning".

Not knowing what to do, wondering how to react, not wanting to hurt her, much impressed by her love and care, he quietly obeyed her orders and lay down on the tattered sheet and went off to sleep. Gujjari also slept on the ground putting her head under the feet of Kanha. She felt as if she was in heaven. Kanha had come to her hut and nothing could be better than that. She was so fortunate to have him. His presence made her completely forget all that disturbed her. With such thoughts of joy and peace running in her mind, soon she was fast asleep, snoring.

Night passed, Kanha heard the temple bells ring in the early hours of the morning. He got up a little confused thinking "what will happen if those pandits do not find me in the temple". He was slightly disturbed and looked at Gujjari who was fast asleep with her head under his feet. He loved her so much, whose very soul was full of love for him. He carefully and quietly got up making all efforts not to wake her up and so compensate for the day long agony that she had gone through. He in a hurry snatched whatever came in his hands as his 'pitambari', put it on himself and ran out of the hut softly closing the door behind him. He reached the temple few minutes before the pandit opened the door of his room. The pandit as usual started cleaning the floor. But when he glanced at the idol, he was shocked. In the place of 'pitambri' Kanha was wearing at night, there was a new blue "dupatta". He tried hard to recollect if the mistake was not committed by him. But sure, next moment, he recalled that there was no such 'dupatta' in Kanha's collection of clothes. He was definite that such a mistake was not possible. He wondered if Kanha had gone out shopping and brought this blue coloured 'dupatta', perhaps getting fed up of the yellow 'pitambri' that He had to put on for all times, day in and day out. But then the shops were closed. Did He then ask some one to open the shop for He wanted to get a new 'dupatta'. All types of thoughts ran within him as he stood before the idol puzzled and confused. Nothing satisfied him as he was unable to get a clear answer. Wondering what to do, he went out and called in other pandits to see what had happened. All were taken aback. All round noise was made in the temple. At last the owner was called in. But none could offer a sensible solution to the problem. Apprehensions rose high but with no satisfactory answer.

In the hut Gujjari got up from her sleep and found that Kanha had quietly left her. She was highly annoyed with him, as he never cared to wake her up, else she would have given him his share of morning milk. Thinking that he must not have gone far off and wanting to persuade him to come back, she got up to run out to catch him. She bent down to pick up her 'dupatta'. But she saw what came in her hand was Kanha's worn out ' pitambri'. She spread it out to make sure what she saw before her. Gujjari then paused and a whole current of thoughts ran within her. She was quick to make out the cause of Kanha's moving off without making any noise or disturbing her. She knew as her father had often lovingly told her that her Kanha was a "chor". That was his habit. He would quietly enter the house of the gopis and take away butter, curd or milk or whatever he could get there and then had a nice time eating and enjoying all these things with his companions. That habit must have continued. Once again anger rose within her.

Analyzing the situation, she came to the conclusion that Kanha saw her new 'dupatta' and was clever enough to exchange his worn out 'pitambri' with her new blue 'dupatta'. Poor Gujjari had taken lot of pains to buy it. She got it only two days before from the village fare. To lose her new apparel was too much for her. The loss was unbearable. She was furious. She took the 'pitambri', quickly closed the door of the hut and ran out to settle the matters with her Kanha. It was drizzling and hard winds were blowing, but nothing at the moment could stop her, her anger rose high every minute. She put her 'ghanghri' a little high up and waded through the waters of the river. She could walk only slowly but thoughts ran fast within her. "Kanha is like that, but let me see what he has done with my pretty 'dupatta'. I hope he has not thrown it away. In that case I will scold him before others and ask him to get one for me. What if he is standing there putting on my 'dupatta', I will then exchange it. I will also tell every one of his old habits that my father told me about him. I will fight with him. This old 'pitambri' is of no use for me. But my dress he can use for a good long time". Thoughts rushed within her one after the other, the basis of which was only her immense love for her dear Kanha.

When the pandits made a good deal of noise, Kanha saw what mistake he had committed while coming out in haste from Gujjari's hut. He could also see very well his Gujjari's reaction. But Kanha loves each and every emotion that rises in the heart of one whom he loves. If it is anger, he can sweetly beg for forgiveness. If it is loss he can heartily laugh and run off. He can honour all that springs from true love for him. He was quite amused and waited patiently for what could come next.

The rains had stopped and Gujjari came out of the river, stamped her foot on the ground to dry her self and put her dress and her hair a little in order. She ran fast towards the temple gate. Darban stopped her. She shouted back,

"I have not come to your temple, I have come to settle accounts with my Kanha".

"Have you gone mad?" darban shouted back.

"Yes, I have gone mad, because severe loss makes one so", retorted Gujjari showing her eyes that were enlarged due to her anger.

Darban stood puzzled and speechless, really not understanding what she meant, merely looking at her face in astonishment.

She pushed him aside and ran inside towards Kanha's room.

In the room of Kanha, she saw so many standing there. She wondered why they were all there. Had they come to see if she dared to come there? She did not bother, and looked at her Kanha who was as usual standing there and smiling putting on her new 'dupatta'.

"I know you Kanha, gopis loved you as 'chor' and that

is what you are. You were clever enough to walk out of my hut quietly as you had planned to carry my new 'dupatta' and instead leave your old worn out 'pitambari' for me. Gopis might have tolerated you but on my part I cannot bear such a heavy loss. So then take your 'pitambri' back and give me my "dupatta" immediately".

So saying she gave 'pitambri' to the pandit and requested him to bring back her "dupatta".

All stood stunned and speechless. The owner then came up and said,

"Well, Gujjari, if Kanha is so fond of your blue "dupatta" let Him have it for the day. Next day you can take it back and return His 'pitambri' to Him".

"On your assurance I can do that, Baba" replied Gujjari.

"But I would like to know, how you got this 'pitambri', it is the one He was wearing last night", the owner asked.

"Late evening, yesterday he came to my place" replied Gujjari.

"For what?" asked the owner perplexed.

"Baba, these pandits had treated me harshly. They had held me by my hair and had slapped me. As if that was not enough they threw me out of this place and further they ordered the darban to never allow me to enter this temple", replied Gujjari.

"But why?" asked Baba.

"You have not come to know about all this?" Gujjari asked in surprise.

"Not at all. These pandits never told me anything" replied Baba.

"How can they tell you because they were at fault? They always hold a grudge against me but I do not care.

Yesterday morning it rained heavily and harsh winds were blowing, as a result of which the thin cloth that covered my jar blew off. The small fishes that grow in numbers during the rains, with the rise in the tide due to the harsh winds fell into my jar. Baba, I can on oath assure you that I was absolutely unaware of this. As I poured the milk from my jar into pandit's vessel those fishes jumped out. I was myself taken aback. Do you think I can ever bring such milk for my Kanha? I love him and care for him. But they beat me and insulted me. I tried to explain my position, but they refused to hear me. Kanha was much grieved at their behaviour. As poor Kanha is not allowed to speak in the temple, he came to my place. I was very angry with him. I had not taken a morsel of food for the whole day and was down in bed sobbing", narrated Gujjari.

"But why is Kanha not allowed to speak in the temple?" asked the owner.

"I do not know, but that is what Kanha told me when he came to my place" replied Gujjari "and I can assure you he never tells lies".

Baba was quiet for some and then asked

"Gujjari what happened afterwards?"

"Yes, Baba, late in the evening Kanha came. He tried to console me. He was very sorry for all that had happened in his very presence. He told me that even he had not taken anything since morning. So we both took bread and milk together. He was about to go when it started raining heavily. I stopped him from going in that bad weather. So he went out in the morning when I was asleep. He had designs to take away my new blue 'dupatta' so he left without waking me up".

Gujjari then stopped and asked, "But, Baba, I am

surprised why you did not ask all this from your Kanha".

The owner bent down to touch her feet. Gujjari stepped back saying "Baba, what are you doing! I am so humble and so small before you". But the owner had realized that this simple, small and humble girl was really great, for Kanha Himself went to her lowly hut to console her. They had wrongly held themselves high in their own estimation. They stood nowhere in comparison to this simple, poor girl. They had failed to see the real Kanha behind the idol of the temple, which this girl could feel and see and offer her heart to Him. He remembered the words of Kabir as he looked at Gujjari.

"When you really look for me
You will see me instantly
You will find me in the tiniest house of time".

Gujjari, with her simple, sincere and loving heart found Kanha, which none of them could with their learning, knowledge and all their services that they performed in the temple.

The owner gave orders that Gujjari must be treated with love and respect. No one would ever dare to stop her from coming to the temple. He told the pandits that they must allow her to give milk to her Kanha with her own hands. Gujjari was very happy and bowed before the owner as a gesture of thanks to him. She then got ready to go out. But before that she glanced at her Kanha who smiled and said,

"So, Gujjari, as promised I have made arrangements not only to meet you every morning but also to take milk from your hands. You see I never make false promises."

Gujjari replied with a mischievous smile,

"Well in return I have allowed you to use my pretty blue 'dupatta' for a day". She then went out.
The owner after she had gone off gave orders that on that particular day of every week not only Kanha but all the deities of the temple will be dressed up in the BLUE. This would be a mark of remembrance and respect for Gujjari.. Even Priti who had been listening to the life history of Gujjari, was overwhelmed and she remembered and now understood the words of her own father that he often repeated:
"Love Him as you love me. Feel His presence".

The Sadhu stopped with his eyes gone wet, but with a broad smile on his face said,
"I hope you have got the answer to your query".
"I have got much more than that, Baba. I am really grateful to you".
Priti got up, touched his feet and walked out.

□

In the Neighbourhood

The house next to Priti was sold out. Those who entered it much attracted her attention. There was a grown up boy, who would sit in the verandah on his broad chair and playd with toys placed before him in a basket. He looked on here and there. A grand old lady, who Priti presumed must be his mother, was usually by his side. It seemed she was much occupied by her devotional services as was suggested by the sound of the cronch and the ringing of the bells every day. There were quite a few attendants that looked after them with sincerity. All looked quite strange and unusual and Priti being of inquisitive nature wanted to know all about them. So one day she ventured to enter their house and say, "Hello, Mrs. Vadvani, I have come to ask you if you need something as I am your next door neighbour. My name is Priti and I am a teacher in a college of Delhi University".

"Thank you for your concern. But I may tell you that I was also a teacher in a college here and was teaching English", politely replied Vadvani.

"By the way I am also teaching English", said Priti.

"At the moment I am leading a retired life, quiet and peaceful in the service of my Mother Divine and my son" Vadvani commented.

"But we belong to the same community and I am sure

we shall have a great time together", replied Priti.
"This is my son Gaurav" Vadvani turned and asked her son, "Gaurav say hello to auntie". Gaurav slowly and quietly extended his hand which Priti came forward and took warmly and shook smiling. Vadvani then said "Now say Jai Mata". Gaurav being in a good mood quietly followed his mother's order and folded his hands.
"He does not speak?" asked Priti.
"No" replied Vadvani and spoke philosophically and emotionally, "Life is a sacred mystery, singing to itself and dancing to its tunes, telling tales".
Priti was greatly impressed by her words and said "If you don't mind, I would like to know all about Gaurav and definitely also about you".
"Ours is a long story of ups and downs and cannot be told in a few minutes" sighed Vadvani
"Now Mrs. Vadvani, that you will be here and I will be here we shall be meeting quite often, I would love to sit by your side, to play with Gaurav and to know from you all that had happened in all these years as Gaurav has grown up to be a handsome young fellow, as I can see him now" said Priti.
"Yes, when he sits relaxed, looking here and there, no body can say that there is anything wrong with him" replied Vadvani.
"This is very true, even I felt so when I first saw him" said Priti.
"That reminds me of an interesting incident" said Vadvani.
"Do tell me" pleaded Priti.
"Once it so happened that my husband and myself had gone for shopping and had taken Gaurav with us. We

parked the car and got down to get something from those selling on the roadside. We had hardly crossed the road, when a policeman came up to the car and seeing Gaurav sitting quietly said to him,
"Sir, move the car a little to the right".
Gaurav looked at his face as he talked to him and then quietly turned his face on the other side, spread his legs, put his head comfortably on the back and sat relaxed. The policeman was highly annoyed by his behaviour and on seeing us come up to the car, complained,
"Look at this gentleman sitting inside. When I came to him and requested him to drive the car a little away, he looked to the other side, relaxed and never bothered about what I said".
We smiled, said sorry, got into the car and drove off. So Priti many mistake him like that when he sits quietly. His elder brother who had the habit of swinging on the branches of the trees and running about wildly all over when he was young was usually taken by them as mentally retarded and not Gaurav as they saw him sitting quietly relaxed. Poor Gaurav, he is a tragic case", quietly commented Vadni.
Priti took leave and went off. But she could not rest. She was too curious to know all about them.

Priti would often peep in from her verandah always looking for an opportunity to come and sit by the side of Vadvani and talk to her and when she found one, she never missed it. One day as Vadvani and Gaurav sat alone, she quickly dropped in, shook hands with Gaurav and sat by the side of Vadvani and said,
"Helloo, Mrs. Vadvani, you promised to tell me all about Gaurav. I would love to hear about him. I am very much

interested in knowing all that you would tell me so I will keep on coming to you off and on and find you in a mood to talk about him and surely about yourself".

Vadvani smiled and said, "You are asking me to go back and live again all those moments that I have gone through and which I wish to forget as they are quite painful for me to remember".
"Have you forgotten them?" asked Priti.
"Not really, how can I?" replied Vadvani.
"I am sure you will be slightly relieved by passing them on to me" suggested Priti.
"Oh really, how can I pass them on to you?" asked Vadvani.
"Because, from now on I shall be here to help you all the time" said Priti.
"So you are determined to hear all about Gaurav and his life so far". said Vadvani.
"Yes of course" said Priti.
Trying hard to remember, Mrs. Vadvani began.
"I remember Gaurav was born a very pretty child as his nurse commented when he made his first appearance in this world. But my mother who sat by my side told me, "The child cried for the whole night after his birth, something unusual for a new born child". Perhaps, as I now see, he then knew the tough time that he was going to have in this world. He was aware of the painful and arduous life that lay before him which he would have to live. Life is really a riddle, an unsolved riddle". Vadvani was quiet for some time and then she began again.

"When he was one month old he came to Jamshedpur

where he was a very normal child. Neighbours would come to play with him. He had lovely big eyes and when he opened his mouth to laugh all of us laughed with him. Sitting in his cradle, waving his tiny hands, he would entice all to stop and play with him for a while. I never had the slightest feeling that because of this child, I will be challenged, battered, tried and put down. I will meet hurdles that will break me for this is a very tough world. My courage and my conviction would be my only assets with which I would move on.

But all was well with him for ten months after which as the elders say, some curse fell upon him. It was a bolt from the blue, when after a very slight attack of measles he started having convulsions and what was worse he forgot all that he had learnt in the last ten months. I took him to an eminent doctor, a child specialist of Calcutta, who assured me that it was all because he was in his teething period and he would be fully cured. He worked very hard for him for two months but then finally gave up. Being the youngest child he got all my attention. My heart broke to see him going down each day. All types of magical performances were also tried on him but all of no avail. I broke down completely. Perhaps my condition needed a spiritual anchor but none came my way". Vadvani commented as she took a deep breath.

"Gaurav was two years old when I came to Delhi" Mrs. Vadvani started again.

"So you have been here for a good long time" said Priti

"Yes, I have changed four places before I came to this place, an accommodation which my younger son bought for me. Gaurav is now forty-five years old and you can well understand the trials and tribulations that he has gone through, not only for himself but for his brothers and sister, mother and father. He had darkened their world. But all of us have moved with courage and determination to help him as each one of us could. Though the ultimate responsibility has fallen on my shoulders".

"Mrs. Vadvani, are you trying to put things in brief and quickly conclude your story? But I will not let you do that. I would like to hear in details about Gaurav as he grew up from day to day" said Priti.

"The first place that Gaurav came was Central Vista, a building allotted to army officers, near India Gate, now demolished. The rooms were large and I had three big rooms together with verandas in front and at the back. Gaurav, one year old, would keep on running from one place to another with his attendant behind him so that he did not fall and hurt himself. Restlessness of the brain made him physically restless. One night, during summer, when we were fast asleep in the verandah, he woke up and as usual started walking. He walked without knowing the way and reached the stair case. He put a step forward and went down rolling on the stairs creating a loud sound. A neighbour brought him and woke us up and told us his story. After that we never slept in the verandah, as his safety was in question and also because it was connected to all others. I remember once when I had gone to teach, his attendant got busy talking to another maid, Gaurav quietly got out of his pram and climbed the wall trying hard to sit on it when he lost his balance and fell down. It was quite high as we stayed on the first floor. It would have meant death for a child of three years. But it astonished all as he got up after the fall and started walking. I was informed. I ran home, took him to the hospital where the doctor told me that he was perfectly fine.

Gaurav's only work was to shout and run. No one could stop him from this. He was never violent. He never knew how to hit anyone, even if some one hit him. On getting hurt, he would cry in helplessness for a few seconds and then start again running and shouting as usual. He ate only if someone put the morsel in his mouth.

Priti, life is a polarity. Before his birth there was only brightness all round, for me. I was so happy. I was very social, busy making numerous friends, throwing parties, entertaining men and women, enjoying and moving ahead, talkative, careless too sure that this would be my world and nothing could ever change it. But then with this child, the worse that one could imagine happened. There was nothing but darkness that surrounded me. All started shunning my company, avoiding me. It is important to cultivate love and compassion for such beings as Gaurav, instead he was looked upon with disdain and hatred. What was his fault? What was my fault? Mrs. Vadnvai then stopped and in a reflective mood said as tears came in her eyes, "I went through various experiences, ranging from pinpricks, to offensive remarks and to insults that if I had allowed them to go under my skin I would have gone mad and thought of myself as worthless".

Vadvani had to stop as someone called her from inside. Priti then had to leave, to come some other time, for which she waited eagerly. One day seeing her sitting with Gaurav and in a good mood playing with him, she ventured to come and sit by her side. She said, "What happened next to Gaurav?"

"Priti, all types of treatments were given to him. My husband being an astrologer had full faith in the functioning of the stars and their effect on the life of an individual. A pandit from Hoshiarpur duped him by convincing him that stars would show their effect only if he performed a certain puja and gave five tolas of pure gold to him. At once he took out the money from his provident fund, did the puja and gave that amount of gold to him that he wanted and waited for the stars to function. But the stars never moved in the way the pandit told him. He hopefully waited but finally gave up. Gaurav was then taken to a famous vaid, who only dealt with brain problems and had cured many such patients. He treated him successfully as Gaurav's convulsions stopped for a year, but then these convulsions returned with a severe force and he had to give up. He was taken to AIIMS, to Safdarganj and to Panth hospitals but nowhere did he find any relief. It was very difficult on my part to hold him while standing in the queue waiting for my turn. He would shout and try to run out. Naturally he attracted the attention of others, who went on questioning me one after the other "What has gone wrong with this boy?" "What treatment have you given him so far?" "I can suggest you one for I have seen a patient of this type being completely cured". It was quite painful on my part to keep on answering their queries and listening to their advice. I wondered why they could not mind their own business. Disgusted and disappointed by their approach I could stop them by saying "Are you a doctor that I must respond to so many of your queries". Once I sat in such a mood of desperation when one gentleman stopped and put the same query, "What is the problem with this boy?" I lost my patience for I had been answering such queries for a good long time. In anger I merely said, "Are you a doctor". He was silent and moved away. When I entered the doctor's room I saw him sitting in the doctor's seat. I felt very odd, but he smiled back and said "What is wrong with your child, you can now tell me".

All vaids and doctors failed when I happened to walk into the dispensary of a private doctor. He examined Gaurav and said,

"Look here Mrs. Vadvani such patients are a curse and create worse problems as they grow up".

"What then has to be done?" I asked.

"For such patients there are injections that can help them to pass off quietly giving relief to all", he replied looking down.

I was stunned at his suggestion and came out of the clinic quickly. Later on when I thought of him I felt in a way he was very right. But then why do I cling to Gaurav and why am I willing to go through the ordeal? Is it a mother's instinct? But there are so many that throw such children into ashrams, where due to negligence they soon die. What is it that holds me so strongly to Gaurav that I am willing to leave all only for the sake of this child? Is it because of my past sins?" Vadvani was quiet as she put this question to Priti. Poor Priti, she looked on with a blank look at her as she had no answer to give. She could only change the topic and after a while left for her place.

Again finding an occasion Priti entered Vadvani's verandah, shook hands with Gaurav, and sat down by the side of Vadvani and said,
"I often hear you singing sad songs, why?"
"For me who has no voice for singing, singing sad songs often has a way of healing a situation. It gets the hurt outside in the open, into the light, out of darkness and provides great relief" replied Vadvani.
"That is very true" agreed Priti.
"Finding no help from the outside world, I turned to the Divine for some help and started doing a little bit of puja" said Vadvani and continued "I got a strong feeling that this world would definitely help me and provide me great support. The incessant experiences of pain in looking after Gaurav and with no change coming to him, kept on destabilizing me and caused great distress. I loved him and I hated him. "Why" I could not analyse as my day to day experiences were brimming with such happenings. Was there a way out? I wondered.

"Poor boy, Gaurav was engaged to the best of his ability into the play of life fulfilling his role on this earth as desired by God. But by fulfilling his role he became a great nuisance to others. He would run out as soon as he saw the entrance door left open by mistake by anyone. He would rush out on the road, never bothered about what was coming from behind or from the front, whether it was a tonga, a bus, a car, a cycle or anything whatsoever. It was their duty to save him for he had no fear of any thing. He walked straight, confident, and unconcerned. We would run out, as fast as we could, when we found that he was not inside the house. Many incidents happened that assured me that some high power was saving him to live and to suffer. I always wondered if Gaurav knew about it.

I will tell you only a few such instances. Once he ran out and went on the other side crossing the road. The horse of the tonga passing that side hit him and he fell down. We could not reach that side so fast and the tonga driver could not control his horse. Gaurav fell down and the vehicle passed over his body. In dismay and despair we looked on sure that he would be dead. But to the surprise of all he stood up unhurt, looked here and there and started running again. He was then only five years old. His brother ran to catch him. A crowd gathered and to the surprise of all he had not received a scratch even. We bit our fingers as it appeared only a miracle to all of us.

Not long afterwards, once while he was playing on the lawn outside and his attendant was inside someone watching a pretty child so overactive quietly came inside and took him away. When we realized that Gaurav was missing, we ran in all directions to find him, but Gaurav was nowhere to be found. I felt I had lost my treasure. My heart sank. I cried as I continued to search for him in every corner. My other children also ran in various directions. But Gaurav was nowhere to be seen. He disappeared in the morning and till evening there was no news of him. I cursed my fate, for I wished that he ought not to have gone away from me in this manner.

Police was informed, all possible measures were taken but none yielded any result. Disgusted, disappointed, and distressed as I sat, while it had gone dark, a sharp telephone bell again informed me that a child of five had been brought by a sadhu to a nearby police station and I need to come in and see if he was Gaurav. We had been running to various police stations on similar calls that a child of five had come and I must come to see if it was Gaurav. But at every station we were disappointed. It had already gone dark and I was completely worn out so I asked the officer to call the child by his name and let us know if he responds.

He did so and told us, "The child is so disturbed that he hardly responds to anything". Not willing to leave anything to chance, I requested the officer, "Please do not allow the sadhu who has brought him there, to go away". The inspecter replied, "He has found him on the road sleeping and when he woke him up the child clung to him crying. Sensing some foul play he has brought him here". Fast I went, pretty sure that I would again be disappointed. But to my surprise I saw Gaurav sitting on the chair depressed and much confused. I asked for the sadhu, the inspector pointed to the back chair but no one was there. The inspector ran out to see him but he was untraceable. "Last minute he was there", he told me, when he came back and was quite surprised as to how he could have disappeared so fast, in such a short time. I picked up Gaurv with a feeling that I had found my lost treasure. I was overjoyed. I wanted to get rid of him, but at any suggestion that he would go away from me, my heart collapsed. Why? I sat to analayse but failed to get a convincing answer.

Gaurav recognized only one person, and that was his mother, his constant solace in pain, in trouble or in joy. He never bothered for any thing. All was irrelevant for him, clothes, safety, food and looks. He would fall down, bleed, and that would make him cry for a few seconds and then he would forget every thing and he would start on his work of running fast and shouting loudly. Helpless, unconcerned about society or himself he grew up into a handsome young boy. Once his neighbours loved him but now he had turned out to be a nuisance to them. His shouts much disturbed them especially at nights. But I was helpless. Whenever a visitor entered our house, poor Gaurav was pushed inside a room and the door was bolted from outside". Mrs Vadvani sighed and continued,

"What is imperative in such a situation is that one should not get demoralised. The ugly comments of the society always let me down. But the next moment I bravely held to my values and soldiered them. I held my head high and said, 'Say what you may, but you will never erode my self confidence and my self esteem".

"You must be going through such difficult situations quite often", remarked Priti.

"Yes, Priti and they very heavily preyed on my nerves. I remember the time of my daughter's marriage. The marriage procession was about to enter my gates. As usual Gaurav was pushed inside the room and bolted from outside. I forgot to close the door of the attached bath room. Within a few seconds came the sound of a big fall. I rushed to open the room and what I saw, I shudder to recall it. Gaurav stood before me bleeding profusely and blood pouring out and flowing all over his whole face. He had entered the bathroom and slipped there.While falling down, he struck his head against the pipe which opened a deep wound and the blood was flowing out in a stream profusely. A senior nurse, our acquaintance who had been invited to the party told me that bleeding could stop only if the wound was stitched. But that was not possible as the marriage procession was about to enter the gate and I had to be present there. At such a critical time no one would take Gaurav's responsibility. It was a very painful situation for me. But somehow the nurse could manage to save the situation applying her brilliant skill.

"With Gaurav, you must be facing such situations every now and then" commented Priti

Mrs Vadvani took a long breath as her eyes moistened which showed her distress and desperation. I went to Lucknow to attend my brother's marriage and sat inside with Gaurav as the party functions went on. Nobody came forward to hold Gaurav. They only pitied me as they passed by. Disappointed I vowed that I would never come to attend any other marriage and henceforth I never came in any function. Priti, three marriages of my own children were performed in my own house, but I never really enjoyed them. I was always worried about Gaurav, for every moment I feared the next, which I knew would be worse than before". Mrs Vadvani was quiet for sometime as she recalled her past horrors and then began again,

"Priti, on the occasion of the marriage of my younger son, I paid one fellow whom I knew well to look after Gaurav for the evening when I went to attend the reception given to us. When I returned at eleven o'clock at night, I found Gaurav standing at the gate trying hard to escape and that fellow in whose care I had left him fast asleep on the sofa inside. The only consolation was that the gate was bolted from inside and Gaurav could not come out on the street. Someone was definitely saving him on every occasion to live and suffer and involve me in this game in which I too must equally suffer. Don't you think so Priti? At least this is my analysis of the entire game as it unfolded before me". A sharp telephone bell called Vadni inside and Priti left after a warm handhake with Gaurav.

Next time when they met, Mrs. Vadni only talked about her great faith in the divine. "Priti, sometimes when the way ahead is difficult and unclear, faith has helped me to move forward. Looking back I see the grim situations that I have been in but these had taught me priceless lessons. I have learnt not to retaliate when others attacked me. They talked about me, not as Mrs. Vadvani, but as a mad boy's mother. If anyone asked my address they would speak in the same manner. It immensely hurt me but I was quiet. I bore all types of insults that were hurled upon me, silently. It was at this time that I moved into an inhabited other world, when this world as I knew no longer accepted me. Was it that I could reach into our intrinsic divine self and connect to Divinity. Yes, I tried hard to be one with the divine and some what, though very little, I succeeded. I believed in the words of Tagore, who rightly says 'Faith is the bird that feels the dawn breaking and sings while it is still dark'. I tried thus to balance myself and move on with confidence and hope".

When ever Priti got a chance to sit with Mrs Vadvani, she never missed it. In fact she was always on the look out for one. Next time when she sat with her she said, "last time you talked only about yourself. But this time I would like you to tell me more about Gaurav".
Vadvani after thinking hard began,
"Priti, a new treatment of brain by surgery was invented in a foreign country. It had cured many patients like Gaurav. A famous doctor in The Panth Hospital suggested that Gaurav should immediately be taken over there for an operation which would definitely put him right. She would call up that doctor and brief him with Gaurav's case. But financial problems came in my way and she suggested only half heartedly, not assuring very good results, a doctor in the south who was performing the same operation after getting some training in the foreign country. Fast we ran with hopes of recovery for Gaurav.

I visited many temples, taking Gaurav with me and prayed for God's blessings. Few south Indian officers working under my husband, who accompanied me, told me of a saint, the original Shankracharya, who lived, not very far away, and had great healing power. He never sat on the kingly seat but occupied a very lowly place. That was his greatness, but if he chose to bless anyone, even the dying got a new life. They told me, "You could go and try your luck. Miracles happen when spiritual energies create auras that take super human leaps". I quickly agreed to anything that worked for the betterment of Gaurav. My husband always brushed aside any such assurances. Gaurav was nine years old and I took him to the saint to be blessed before the operation was performed. The saint, a thin old man, half naked, sat on a piece of cloth spread on the ground. His looks showed his unconcern about this world. He sat speechless, absentminded, looking here and there. There was an iron railing to protect him from the public. A certain calmness prevailed around him. The officer accompanying me spoke in his south Indian language, begging the saint to bless Gaurav as he was going for a brain operation next day. He heard quietly and then wanting to bless Gaurav, put his hand over a basket of fruits. He wanted to take one out and give it to Gaurav. Believe me Priti, it was a very happy moment of my life. But as luck would have it, his hand got entangled with few strings tied over the basket. He was taken aback as his looks suggested and in consequence of which he took a big turn and looked at Gaurav for few minutes, and then turned completely to the other side, brought his hand away from the basket and sat quietly. Why he did so, what he read in Gaurav's face was a riddle for all of us who were watching him and his movements very closely. We were disheartened as we had come with great hopes. The officer then raising his voice at a high pitch requested, begged and pleaded the saint to bless Gaurav and not disappoint him, but it was all to no avail. He looked to the other side and refused to respond. Depressed and disheartened we returned. The conclusion was clear that the operation would be a failure".

"But Mrs Vadvani what did the saint see in Gaurav's face?" asked Priti

"Perhaps being a saint of a high order as I could see, he could co-relate Gaurav to his previous life and visualized that he must continue to suffer and equally make me suffer, therefore there was no need to give his blessings. If his hand was stuck, there was surely some reason and he found it out on observing Gaurav's face. We were all over confident the way he proceeded but what followed made us highly depressed. Disappointed and dejected we returned with a definite feeling that the operation would not succeed.

Poor Gaurav went through all the agony of the brain operation which turned out to be a complete failure. It was worse than that. His whole body was paralysed. He lay almost dead as there was no movement in his body only his eyes were open and that too with no expression in them, stony and fixed. This made the doctor highly nervous. He ordered for special massages and close monitoring. He himself came twice a day. I shuddered to think that I had to take him back in that state. We lost our temper as the doctor had taken a good amount from us on the promise that he would definitely put him all right. He tried all sorts of treatments on him but was a complete failure. Gaurav lay motionless for a week. Our anxiety grew with each passing day as we were sure that we would finally be asked to take him away in that terrible condition.

A mood of pessimism prevailed. We sat in the verandah on the morning of the eighth day thinking how to take the next step when, we heard some rattling sound coming from inside so we got up to see what it was. We stood highly astonished as Gaurav was there before us running fast in his usual style. We were much relieved and we brought Gaurav home exactly in the same condition as we had taken him, with no change what so ever. I could see the hand of the saint that got stuck when he wished to bless him. I could see that Gaurav was born to live and suffer. I could see that I must also suffer so I was linked so closely to him. I could see the hand of a great power that was always extended to save him to meet more and more disasters". Mrs Vadvani stopped after this comment and was silent for some time. She then said, "When I begin to talk about Gaurav, there seems to be no end to it. But I have some urgent work and I must go". She excused herself and went in.

Mrs. Vadvani's life appeared so strange and so interesting to Priti that she eagerly waited for the next occasion when she could sit by her side and say, "What next, Mrs. Vadvani". It was only after a good long time that she saw from her veranda Vadvani sitting in a good mood playing with Gaurav. Priti quietly walked in, shook hands with Gaurav and sat by the side of Vadvani "How are you Mrs. Vadvani? I have not seen you for long. I hope everything is all right?"

"I was a little busy these days in my writing work" replied Vadvani with a smile.

"I just wanted to hear more about Gaurav. Do tell me if you are in a mood to do so", Priti pleaded.

"Priti, to continue, my husband retired and the grand bungalow that we had acquired for the last twenty years had to be vacated. I had a strong feeling that Gaurav could not live in a small house for he wanted good space to run about. So I bought a large area far off from the city on which a huge bungalow was constructed. It was due to the lack of funds that I had to run off to a distant place far removed from the city. Here was a place where

Gaurav ran about freely. There was no need of any one to run after him. If he fell, he was not hurt for all around there was soft grass. Once we had gone out for shopping to the city early in the morning leaving Gaurav with a servant whom we had recently engaged. He took out all the money from my cupboard and left, leaving Gaurav all alone. When I returned late in the evening, I saw Gaurav sitting on the verandah on a bed with a very strange expression of exhaustion on his face. I called out for the servant but he was no where to be found. I came out and enquired about him from the neighbours who told me that they had seen him going out in the morning, carrying a bag with him. I am sure that we would have found Gaurav dead because, he had to be looked after every minute and I wondered who saved him and cared for him the whole day.

"But anyhow for Gaurav it was a very convenient place and I was much relaxed, though for my college I had to change three buses. It was very tiring, but I was happy. My husband, however, found the lack of electricity a curse. The supply was erratic. He was highly disturbed because he found it a great hindrance in his studies of astrology, in his readings and writings and watching T.V. The jolt of recent retirement, loneliness, and lack of good neighbours made the matters worse for him. He took to heavy smoking which brought about his sudden death. It was for me a very harsh blow. I was also nearing my retirement and we could have lived here peacefully. But his death came as a severe shock which completely paralysed me. The thought of being left alone to steer the ship of life carrying the burden of Gaurav made me go mad. His presence was a great consolation. At least we were two to share each other's grief. I cried bitterly, no consolation worked. But then that was not the solution.

"In such a desperate state I even lost my faith in the Divine, to which lately I had dedicated myself. My Mother Divine, I hated Her for She could have allowed my life to run as it was running. But no, She went ahead to make it worse for me. For what then She should have a place in my home and in my heart? I threw Her out of my heart, out of my mind and out of my house in sheer disgust and despair and went to occupy a small rented house with my son who had come to support me, at this critical time, leaving his job. For me there was nothing but sufferings. They say in life if there is darkness there is also light. But my case was an exception, where there was nothing but darkness with no light ever shining. Already suffering from the setback of Gaurav, here was a more severe blow. I lost my peace, I lost my faith and I lost my patience. I was a complete wreck.

"I was going through sleepless nights and turbulent days, when I was taken to a psychiatrist who diagnosed my disease as severe depression and prescribed pills to be taken that would give rest to my disturbed mind. All who met me asked when they looked at my face only one question "What has gone so wrong with you?" They also suggested that troubles do come in life. I refused to talk to them and moved on. I was moving aimlessly and anxiously. Life is a movement and movement needs a guide. I had lost all guides, spiritual, mental and physical. The storm was brewing up and the ship moved unbalanced.

I had never heard that Gods are helpless. Great teachers had taught me that if you surrender yourself to Him, He takes good care of you. I had full faith in my Mother Divine, but even She had deserted me. Anguish, pain and anger made me mad. I had thrown Her out from my mind and from my heart and from my very self. No longer any puja room was needed as I had stopped all puja which I found was no good. I had left behind, Her photograph that I loved once for concentration to reach to some higher level. Turmoil was within me as it twisted and turned every part of my body and my very spirit. A severe churning within me took place as I tried to normalise myself and move forward in my life to take care of Gaurav. It was so difficult. I faltered at every step. Disturbance within led me to sleeplessness. Pills could have helped me, but if I slept who would take care of Gaurav? Then a miracle happened". Vadvani stopped.

"Why have you stopped? I am curious to know about your miracle, for it must have changed your life. Do continue", pleaded Priti in all earnestness.

Vadvani thought for a while and then said, "I really cannot describe that experience. I cannot do full justice to what I felt and did. I will try to recollect and then let you know next time when we are together".

"Please Mrs. Vadni, begin telling me and I am sure you will recollect. I will help you. I am so eager to hear strange things. I am not moving out", insisted Priti.

"How are you going to help me, when you were not there with me. Even if you were there you could not have guessed what moved within my heart and changed my entire world?" asked Vadvani quite amused at Priti.

"I am not going away and I must hear about your miracle", reiterated Priti.
"If you are adamant I have to tell you" replied Vadvani taking a deep breath, "really not doing full justice to what went on within me at that moment". Vadvani was quiet for some time and then she began.

"One day, Priti, I was searching for a broom to clean the dust that had gathered under Gaurav's bed. I saw quite a number of them put on a shelf in the verandah. I pulled out one amongst many that were kept there. As I took it out, I saw something colourful that sparkled from below. Curious to find what it was, I removed a few brooms and saw to my surprise the big photograph of my Mother Divine, which was kept there to give a solid support to the brooms. My heart throbbed and I could not control the tears that came in my eyes as a voice spoke within "How dare you come here. I had given strict orders that you should not come here as I threw you out. Yet you are here. You had heaped upon me disaster after disaster yet you are not willing to leave me". While the brain thus argued, somewhere in the corner of my heart a shrill voice rose to say something quite different, "Remember me for I never forget you". I moved fast to take her out from beneath the grooms, cleaned her with my pulloo, searched for a small room and lovingly placed her on a neat shelf.

With tears in my eyes and folded hands as I stood before Her, I said, "I am sorry, Ma, I have blundered under the weight of my sorrow. Perhaps I could not throw you out completely from my heart. So you are here without my wanting you to be so. You loved me more than I loved you. But forgive me once for all that I have thought and done".

Ma replied, "When you come to me with tears, I am really pained, but at times I am helpless, for there are things that have to come as destined. Let not the troubles break you, you need to break the troubles. I can give you my assistance, infuse you with courage to act bravely in life. You have determination, you have courage, so hold your head high and move on, remembering that I am always behind you".

"Once again, Priti, I started my puja, and you would not believe that sleep came running to me as soon as I picked up my mala at night. I got up from the bed fresh in the morning to go to my college and attend to my daily rounds. Ever since then She has provided me with courage to move on in life facing troubles with a smile. The song of the heart is the pure voice of heaven. It became strong within me. I had refused to listen to it, but it came up with a redoubled sound and a big bang. I now do meditation during the very early hours of the morning. I am alone, absolutely alone. I sit by the side of Gaurav and look into the darkness and move into it. The beauties and significance of this time is not known to many. It is the right time for meditation when I try to move to Her. She could not be found in noise and restlessness. She is the friend of silence. We need silence to touch the soul.

"Peace cannot be had by force. It comes only through understanding. I had understood well by this time that Gaurav had to suffer and remain like that. I also understood well that I may cry as much as I liked, my husband will not come back. The Divine gave me this lesson. I tried to control my mind, for if you overcome your mind, you overcome the world because mind is the root cause of all that one experiences in this world. It was only when my mind, put in the right direction, that I became happy and satisfied. I left this world of comfort and went into a world of intuition and what I found was wonderful. I discovered that life means challenges and I had to face in my life many challenges however severe they may be. It had brought me face to face to a strange realization, a realization that made me discover my self. I was happy with what I found. I simply looked at life in a new way. I tried to laugh and change, and when I changed the whole world changed around me. I created a new world that I deserved. I became optimistic as I believed in the power of my faith, for faith can move mountains.

"Hence forth I never complained about Gaurav. No more shutting him in a room as visitors entered the house. Instead I proudly introduced Gaurav as my youngest son living with me. Gaurav would either shake hands with them or would quietly fold his hands to mutely say 'jai Mata'. All would stop to say a few words to him or would lovingly touch him. I was no longer ashamed of him as I was once upon a time.If someone chose to comment adversely on Gaurav or on me, I refused to pay any heed to it. I became firm as I was happy with my lot. Gaurav to me was no curse, but a part of my life, a part of myself that I loved the most".

Priti then remarked, "Mrs. Vadvani, I see good

attendants that are by the side of Gaurav".
"Yes," Vadni nodded "that is a great blessing. They say that it is the way that God serves and helps. He takes their form to make our lives easy. There has been a great variety amongst them and I have learnt a lot through them about human nature and human problems. I had a businessman who had lost all in his business and had nothing to fall back upon, a tribal who had been running through mountains, and in jungles and had led a very odd life there, an old mother deserted by all her four sons and the best, one who had murdered his neighbour, dug him deep into the earth and had run away from the police to this distant place and had come to serve Gaurav. But I must say they were all very sincere and good to us. Even the present lot is sincere and reliable and they have been with us for a good long time".

Vadvani hearing a sharp telephone bell ring, went inside and Priti left for her home. Next time when they met both were in a jovial mood. Vadvani said,
"Priti, I had a strong feeling that Gaurav could never be cured after what the saint indicated. The events that followed were in the same direction. Despite that I was unwilling to believe in this truth. I had hopes beyond hope that Gaurav would be cured one day. I went through devices, secretly, irrational as they were, thinking that they might act like miracles which others did not believe in. I ran for anything that I was given to understand would do wonders not understood by others. When I think of them now, I feel amused and at times ashamed".
"Do tell me those devices as I love to hear anything about Gaurav" said Priti

"You know Priti, behind the madness was a heart of a mother too full for one who entirely looked at her in sheer helplessness and pain", remarked Vadvani.

Priti insisted, "But do tell me those devices that you took".

"But you promise not to laugh at me", said Vadvani.

"Please go on" Priti requested.

"One day Gaurav's attendant brought some one who had seen Gaurav while he was on his evening stroll. The attendant told me,

'Here is some one who promises to cure Gaurav ji'

I looked at the stranger who said,

'My master had been roaming amongst the Himalayas, from where he has brought very precious roots out of which he had taken out oil, which applied on the head would fully cure the patient. Your son is perfectly all right. It is only the heat in his brain that makes him restless. This oil will cool him down and fully cure him".

"Where is the oil?" I asked.

"My master had opened a shop, where you can come and buy it", replied that stranger.

I immediately rushed to the shop and found a sadhu sitting there, which further impressed me and I asked for the oil. The fellow gave me a bottle.

"What is the cost?" I asked.

"Nothing as compared to the wonders it can do, only thirty thousand rupees", the sadhu replied.

It was too huge an amount for me to carry in the pocket, so I promised to come the next day. If I told about it to my eldest son he would have dissuaded me from buying, so quietly I went to the bank, took out the money and purchased the bottle.

"When will I see the results?" I asked.

"Within a week. Please do come to me after a week and let me know the progress. I can assure you that he will be fully cured by that time" the sadhu assured me.
I applied the oil, religiously on Gaurav's head, but found no change. So after a week I went to the shop and was surprised to find quite a number like me were sitting and making similar complaints. But to our disgust and dismay the shop was closed. On enquiry we were told that the fellow had left forever without telling where he was going to open the shop next to fool people like us".
Priti had a hearty laugh.
"I told you not to laugh. You know Priti, when a delicate chord of the heart is touched one rushes into any madness, because the brain has stopped working for the time and the heart is leading one into blunders after blunders", said Vadvani.

I stepped into a place where the healer believed that mental patients suffer when a bad spirit enters the body and captures the soul. It makes the person restless. Naturally the remedy was to free the person from this evil. The healer gave some drink that would make the spirit speak. It would then be beaten and thrashed so that it would leave the body thus providing relief to the mental patient.
There was a big hall. I peeped into it and what I saw sent tremors in my body. It was full of men and women who were shaking their bodies and twisting their heads. They were uttering non sense. Woman with their open hair waved it all round. I was shocked to see it. I retraced my steps and asked,
"What is going on here?"

"The ghosts within them are shouting. After a good beating they will tell their stories. Accordingly they will be treated and thrown out". The healer replied.

"You will make Gaurav also to speak out?" I asked.

"Definitely, the ghost within him has to tell his story before it is taken out", he emphasized.

"If you can make Gaurav speak, I can pay you handsomely" I remarked.

"Sure, no problem", he gave an assurance as he roughly caught Gaurav's hand and dragged him towards the hall.

While taking him to give the drink, my heart sank and I ran with him.

"But listen,Gaurav is dumb and cannot speak. Are you sure that you can make him to talk?" I asked.

Fast he dropped Gaurav's hand and said, "In that case I am helpless. If the ghost within him is not going to tell me how and when it entered, I can neither satisfy nor beat that ugly ghost".

I came back at least for once saved from putting Gaurav to an unnecessary harassment.

"I wonder, being so intelligent and so highly educated you could even think of such methods for Gaurav well understanding his problem" said Priti in sheer disgust.

"In pain you are apt to lose your balance and run for anything that promises relief", sighed Vadvani.

"I was told about a woman who presumed that there were insects in the brain which could be taken out through the ears and thus successfully dealt with the mental problems. I was quick enough to get the address and fast reached the place. The old woman who was giving the treatment surprised me by taking out big, black insects from Gaurav's ears. My hopes rose high soon to be dashed down. I could see more harm than good that was done here.

"I was taken to a man of hundred years who was still strong, working hard even at his age of hundred years, only by doing exercises daily. He assured me that he would cure Gaurav only through exercises. I was quite impressed. He made Gaurav do such hard exercises forcibly that he cried doing it and had very severe convulsions for the whole night. I left him in despair.

Gaurav walked all the way to Vaishnav Devi, which surprised the pandits there who took him inside to bless him. It was long back when he was small only of the age of seven. He went to Balaji to get darshan. He himself steered though the crowd and stood before the Idol of Balaji, where the pandit stood, who fast came forward to give Gaurav, the blessings of Ballaji. He then was taken to Ttiputi Maharaj where he was picked up from the crowd by the pandit, brought before Triputi Maharaj and offered special blessings. As I always accompanied him because he was small, I was also lucky to get the blessings of so many Gods and Goddesses. We went to many other temples but it appeared that all were not in a mood to help my Gaurav and me. My own puja, though it gave great solace to me brought no relief to Gaurav.

But often the throb of the heart silenced the voice of the mind for the time being and I continued to try every device that came before me. I never got discouraged for I felt it is often the last key in the bunch that opened the lock. I was on an arduous journey of trials and errors, always optimistic that better fate awaited me and Gaurav. Even now I do not cry that it all happened. I moved on with a smile. Nothing, medicines, turning to new doctors, strange devices and prayers brought any relief to Gaurav. He ran and ran, he shouted, he fell and broke his head, cried for a while and then again went on to his usual routine.

I had learnt by this time that challenges must be taken bravely. I fought with them courageously to conquer. But then if I failed and the situation did not change I had also learnt to accept everything with grace and dignity. Gaurav was mine, is mine and will ever remain mine. I smiled and took all my troubles as God's wish. Problems that I have faced had shown me a new path to follow. I now move on in my life with confidence in myself, head held high, faith in God and a smile for all. I am happy with my lot whatever it is. I remain calm and quiet so much so that others often envy me".

Priti was quick to respond, "But Mrs. Vadvani, Gaurav neither runs nor shouts".
"Oh, yes Priti, that brings me to the last great event that happened in his life. But I will let you know some other time as I am quite tired now", said Vadni.
"Sure, Mrs. Vadni, we will keep it for the next turn", Priti got up, smiled, shook hands with Gaurav and left for her house.

Next time when Priti sat by the side of Vadvani, Priti as usual pleaded, "You promised to tell me something more about Gaurav". "Oh, yes" Vadvani smiled and began,

"It was a terrific time that Gaurav and all of us had. An incident that redoubled my faith in my Mother Divine and an occasion that marveled others. Govrav was having fever for sometime. I asked his doctor, under whose treatment he was at that moment if I should bring Gaurav to him for examination. He was silly enough to say, "There is nothing serious to worry about. Every time the fever comes up you can give him a tablet of crocine". The fever started coming frequently and every time I would ring him up, he would tell me the same thing. I did as I was told. But something very serious was going on within Gaurav, which of course he could not tell and which I completely failed to understand. On one evening he became slightly restless, the reason for which I could not make out. By night this restlessness increased immensely and I found he could not breathe easily. Gaurav would run out of his bed and cried painfully in his effort to breathe. It came up vehemently by late night and continued to increase with every passing moment. Nothing serious has happened to Gaurav so far. So I failed to understand him completely. But by this time I could see that there was something dangerous brewing within him. It was late night and I could not call any doctor. I remained a helpless on looker who could merely sit, weep at his worsening condition and watch on. The whole night I sat by his side, waiting for the morning to come, wondering all the time why the morning was taking such a long time to come. Morning arrived after an anxious wait. I took him to his doctor, who to my surprise told me to take him immediately to a hospital as he had little time left for him. I was stunned at his words. But losing no time, he was taken to a nearby hospital, where the doctor after examination fast put him into a ventilator. My heart sank, for I knew that no one comes out of it alive.

So Gaurav lay in an I.C.U. in a ventilator with strings tied and needles poked into his body. There was no movement, only his eyes were open and whenever I was allowed to see him, tears would run out of his eyes, calling me out to tell that he was suffering immensely. "Gaurav is technically dead" one doctor attending him told me.
"But then why are you keeping him here?" I asked.
"Because he is still breathing" he replied.

His eldest brother ran and was willing to give all to save him. He forgot his job, forgot his self and all his comforts. He was by his side day in and day out. All night he woke in the hospital. At the slightest provocation, he would get serious and much disturbed. He was willing to give his blood and spend all that he had. He never hesitated to give money for the life saving pills, costing one lac each, prescribed by the doctor, as the last resort to save Gaurav. The younger brother on hearing about Gaurav's illness came running from Washington. He took the permission from the authorities to stand by his side every morning to chant mantras and pray for his recovery. My daughter stood by my side so was my youngest sister.

There were those who told me, "Gaurav's very existence has been a heavy burden for you as well as for him. If he goes away it would be a great relief to you both. It is your love and your prayers that are saving him and not allowing him to exit. If he goes off, it would be a great relief to you, one, who has suffered so much on account of him".

Yes, what they said was very true. But at their very suggestion tears would flow out of my eyes and I cried loudly despite my best efforts to control myself and at least appear calm before others. Days passed and nights passed and I kept on fearing every minute that it would perhaps be the last for Gaurav. When I would return home from the hospital the deadly silence that prevailed in the house because Gaurav was not there, glared at me, pierced through my heart and gave me immense pain and the toys that lay scattered all round told me that they would miss the one who was so fond of them and will not be there henceforth. This very thought of the future killed me. I will have to live without Gaurav. I was not prepared for that. I would retrace my foot from moving on into my own house.

Relations and friends thronged to give support. Astrologers were consulted who spoke in one voice that Gaurav's time had come to an end and he must go. Pandits refused to do any Puja as it would be ineffective and would not give any positive results. Doctors had already given the signal that anything could happen any time, though they were doing their best. I groped in this darkness for a period of one month. But there was one streak of light and ray of hope that pulled me up. I wept bitterly in my bed as I lay alone in the darkness of the night. I do not know when I went off to sleep when I saw in my dream my Mother Divine who said sweetly,

"Why are you crying?"

"You are asking something you know well", I replied with tears flowing down my cheeks.

"Now, wipe those tears for I have made my lion to sit just near the window of your room so that you may be guarded against all evils".
She then disappeared before I could speak.

Down somewhere this voice gave me immense courage to move on with hopes, though the realities pointed to the opposite direction and I had to believe in what they had to say. I was in real turmoil. But when my sons asked me,
"What sort of vibrations are you getting?"
I would promptly reply, "despite all the dreaded realities that I am facing, I have very positive vibrations". We took some relief from this feeling and moved forward in all our efforts to save Gaurav.

They say that "prayers can do more than what the world can dream of". Slowly, and silently to the surprise of all Gaurav came out of his ventilator. For the doctors the life saving pills that were given as the last resort worked, but how fast they worked was quite a surprise to them. A patient "technically dead" walked out full of life into the side room and then put in my lap. I was overjoyed. I thanked all that supported me in my distress. But my special thanks go out for my Mother Divine who held up my spirits every minute during this ordeal.

"What happened next, Mrs. Vadvani?" asked Priti.
"After this" replied Vadvani "he is as you see him now. He forgot running. He forgot shouting. His convulsions to the surprise of his doctor looking after his brain and to the surprise of all vanished. He now sits quietly and claps when bhakti songs are played. He abhors any

other music. He is very happy playing with his toys or looking here and there.

Mrs. Vadvani stopped and then said, "Do you know Priti what I feel".
"Of course, if you are willing to share your feelings with me" replied Priti.
Vadvani sighed as she commented, "the greatest curse that a woman can have is to have a mother's heart". She wiped her tears as she went in.

□

Reflections

Priti felt that Vadvani was a very good neighbour. Her views on various topics enlightened her. She loved to sit with her and hear what she had experienced and what her reflections on life and happiness were. Her words and suggestions worked on her as an eye opener and made her think seriously what life ought to be. Once she sat with her and said,

"Mrs. Vadvani, you have lived ninety years of your life, a pretty long time to see and understand this world. I hope you do not mind telling me what you feel about life in this world and be my guide".

Mrs. Vadvani replied,

"For sure, I cannot be anybody's guide, all that I can tell you are the thoughts you need to live with, because right thoughts can change your life".

Priti sprang up and said,

"I shall be too happy to hear whatever you have to tell me".

Vadvani smiled back and said,

"You know Priti people condemn 'ego'. We are told that it is ego that pulls down a person and destroys him, so one needs to learn to destroy it. It is true that man is nothing but ego. But I feel ego has two parts to it.

1. Constructive
2. Destructive

Ego becomes a good tool if you take up the constructive side, at the same time it pulls you down if you have the destructive side. With the positive side of ego comes the determination, the ability to take decision and work towards it. Conversely the negative side of ego can lead you to act with arrogance. This prevents you from thinking objectively and eventually you become a victim of your failings. Such a fate could be avoided by effectively managing our ego.

Priti then asked,
"It all seems to sound so vague that I can hardly understand all that you say. Do give some examples so that it gets fixed in my mind".
Vadvani replied,
"I can give you examples of some whom I met and others about whom I read. In my neighborhood, where I lived before coming to this place, was a judge, who told me his story of how he was a poor boy washing the feet of his master thereby earning his living. He had a great desire to study. So he saved some out of the money he got as his pay, bought books and studied hard whenever he got some time, in the late hours of the evening or at night. Once while washing his master's feet in his drowsiness he pressed the feet a little hard, the master gave him a kick, abused him and turned him out. Disappointed, that he had lost the means to study, he walked out on the road heedlessly, where he was hit by a man going fast on his motor bike and was badly hurt. The man took him to the hospital and cared for him. When he became all right the bike-man asked him, "Why you did not move despite my continually ringing the bell as you chose to walk in the middle of the road".

The boy told him of his disappointment and his intense desire to study and be someone. The bike-man was impressed and said, "Do not worry, for I will make provisions for your studies". The boy was overjoyed. His determination made him work hard. As a camel bears toil and heat, hunger and thirst through the deserts of sand and never faints, so the ego, the determination in him made him work hard as he grew up and went through all the examinations always standing amongst the best. He appeared in a judicial examination and was soon appointed as a judge. His master, who had hit him and thrown him out, once appeared before him for he was convicted for misappropriation of funds. The judge acquitted him and cleared him despite his involvement. He was quite surprised and came to thank him. The judge humbly replied, "This is a small return for the kick you gave me as I washed your feet".

"So Priti, if the destructive ego turned a boy out, the constructive ego made a poor boy a judge".

Priti nodded and said,

"I now understand your statement about ego".

Vadvani continued, "Priti, ego becomes a good tool, provided how you use it. It works both ways. It lifts you up and takes you high, but it can also throw you down as you begin to think too highly of yourself and much above all around you. On the one side if it lifts you up to the heights of passion and extraordinary accomplishment, it can also drown you into the depths of disappointment and delusion into defeat and disaster.

Ganga Ram, a poor ordinary boy in a remote village insulted and thrown out by an officer, with his determination, rose to occupy a higher position than

the officer. Finally he became Sir Ganga Ram. I read about a scientist who had perfected the art of reproducing human genome. He wanted to become immortal, so getting old he produced five figures exactly like his own self. When the angel of death came, he failed to pick up the right one for each was made with precision to look alike. He stood puzzled for some time and then he thought of a trick. He touched the ego of the scientist and said,
"Very good work for the scientist to go so high as to make each figure so identical, but he made a small mistake in this one by turning the nose a little too high".
The real one's ego was touched and he rose up to say,
"Sir this is not a mistake but...........".
The angel sprang and caught him by his neck and took him away. If the constructive side made him rise so high in his scientific attempt, the destructive side brought him to his death and disaster.

"So Priti we need not condemn ego altogether, as it is usually done. The two sides need to be understood and great care must be taken not to fall a prey to the destructive side of it. Priti nodded thoughtfully and said "You have really enlightened me".

Next time when Priti came to sit by the side of Vadvani, she looked at her with eagerness so that she may start telling her something more about life and its problems. Finding her in a good mood she asked,
"We always find ourselves in turmoil and in problems losing our balance and composure. In that case what should we do?"

Vadvani spoke thoughtfully,
"Priti you need to make a strong and a very serious effort to move above your turmoil. Merely thinking and taking a decision will not help you. You need to rise up and work hard towards what you decide. Life is time so you need to time your life. Do not waste your life and your precious time. Do not be like a neglected car that gets its battery discharged because it has been standing for a long time. You need to regulate yourself for you know very well what is right and what is wrong, only that you do not practice it. Practice is a great asset. Move towards good and rise above your circumstances. Do not for a moment get discouraged if you lose. I will advise you to keep before yourself the Japanese dorsal doll as your ideal. In whatever direction you throw, the doll immediately stands up when it falls down on the ground. The problem is not that you fall, but how fast you can get up like the dorsal doll. Things happen, you make mistakes, and you fall. No harm, in fact these mistakes give you the determination to fight and rise high. Try to understand where you made the mistake and rise above it. This is the only way to get out of your turmoil. If you fight with your troubles, only then you will be successful. Try to solve your problems and keep moving on. Do not get discouraged and then disappointed. Do not become helpless and then hopeless. Some way will come out if you only move on. You need to stand firm and steadfast with patience. Lose all but do not lose the courage to meet the most dismal situation in life. Remember the famous line of a poet
'If winter comes can spring be far behind'.
When spring comes, winter goes telling you 'Do not forget me'. Create courage in your life and become one

who makes troubles dance and not you to dance round your troubles. Develop an attitude of gratitude and give thanks for everything that happens in your life, knowing that every step forward is a step towards achieving something bigger and better than your current situation. In the depth of winter, you will finally realise that within you there lies an invincible summer. Every single second is an opportunity to change your life, because in any moment you can change the way you think.

Priti who was listening to Vadvani in rapt attention, was slightly puzzled and asked, "Madam, you are asking for too many things. How will I achieve all this? What you say sounds good but we are apt to fall down under the weight of our defeats and turmoil. From where are we to get that strength that you are talking about?"

Vadvani thoughtfully replied,

"Ask for this strength from the Divine and this inner strength will give all that I am talking about".

Priti responded,

"I believe that is why you do puja".

"Exactly" Vadvani replied "I was also like so many others, drowning myself in my problems and turmoil, leading to defeat and disaster, but it was this Divne power that changed my way of thinking and gave me the strength to stand up again in life. I did so and I am so happy today. Spiritualism, bhakti, loving the Divine is the greatest need of the hour. Loving God needs to extend from self to yourself and further to all round you. Bhkti- duty- karma ought to come in one line. What is bhakti? It is nothing but getting immense courage within you to fight with the worst calamities Kabir very rightly said that bhakti gives a lot of strength to rise above your problems and gives you the power to face the turmoil of your life courageously".

Priti then pleaded, "Do tell me more about bhakti which gives inner strength and also what more it can afford for any one.

Vadvani smiled and began,
"I love to talk upon this subject because I have read a lot about it, experienced it and also met those who have this strength. Spiritualism or bhakti what is it? Apart from providing you with courage it has another important aspect to it. If I am asked to define it, I would say that it is nothing but immense love. All love concentrated is bhakti. Bhakti, as many understand it does not mean confining yourself to meditation, jap, or puja. All this must lead you to have faith in yourself, and love for those around you. Flowers, incense, will not reach you to God. What reaches you to Him is your strength that you gain for doing your karma as puja. Always give some little time to remember the Divine. True religion is not talk, or doctrines or theories. It is the relation between your soul and God. Learn to be happy. There ought to be a proper balance between bhakti and karma. I repeat:
There ought to be a close relation between bhakti and karma. All bhakti without karma will never do as karma without bhakti will never reach you to a point of satisfaction. Through bhakti you gain and develop your inner awareness as to how you can rise above your turmoil and how you can serve others. You have to grow from the inside out. None can teach you, none can make

you spiritual. There is no other teacher but you. The spirit of service comes from serving the Lord. Where this spirit is lacking there cannot be any spirit of service for others. If you make this decision to serve others as the central focus of your life, you will then be in a position to know true miracles. With light and joy in your heart you will gain great satisfaction in life.

"The axis or what we say 'dhuree' on which this world rests is love. It simply means feeling and understanding for each other. If your heart is a volcano, how will you expect flowers to bloom? Learn to get out of your bed remembering the Divine and His kindness as you begin the day. Once upon a time the practice was to make the cocks fight. This practice has been overtaken by men fighting like cocks in politics, in office and in the homes. Fights and politics are the common features of the day. Make bhakti, that is love the pivotal feature of your life and then realize the charm of living. A house whose members grow in love and understanding for each other is far above one where the husband beats the wife and the children learn to grow up with a feeling of hatred. A family however poor, that grows up with members who have a lot of love and understanding for each other is far superior to the one that is rich but the members are at each others' throat. Hitler grew up with pain and could bring in the world only pain and disaster. Lal Bahadur Shastri grew up in a poor loving home but gave to the world two things he got: love and service to all.

"India is full of 'mahatmas and gyanies'. They have given us 'granths'. Their views have guided us in life. Indian philosophy is high and shows us our Indian thoughts. Long years of slavery has destroyed a lot of the very precious things we had, our money, our kohinoor, craft, poetry, music, instruments, literature and what not, the list is pretty long. Yet we have managed to survive and rise up once again. The credit goes to the men of high thoughts that guide us. You cannot reach God by rites and rituals, by pilgrimages or by wealth. Sage Vashishta said to Ram, "God is to be attained by overcoming one's mind". It is the right thoughts that need to be cultivated. You read Ramayan many times and in so doing feel that you are very religious but do you practice in your life any thing emphasized in Ram's life? You read Gita, but have you taken one principle out of it to rule your life? If not, it is just like licking the label on your bottle and never taking its contents. Sages and masters have given us thoughts that need to be realized, which means they must be experienced,which means they must be lived.

Priti I remember Kabir who said 'I was going on a pilgrimage to Mecca when on the way I met God. He scolded me and asked 'Who told you that I am to be found only there?' God, as you must understand, is to be found even in homes where there is love and respect for the parents. If you have their blessings even the evil spell of 'Shani' goes off. Learn to remember a few things that are very important. Your father is higher than the sky for he has wished the best for you and is overjoyed when he sees you rising. His mission is to work for you. Priti in this context I may tell you of an incident told often. Lord Krishna visited the house of his devotee. As he was busy giving bath to his old father, he threw a brick for the Lord and asked Him to sit down and wait, for at that moment he was giving bath to his old father and could not attend to him. The Lord sat down on the brick and lovingly kept on watching his devotee give bath to his father, who then wiped him with a piece of cloth and then wrapped him in a dhoti and made him sit comfortably on the bed. After all the work was done, he turned to the Lord and said 'Sorry for making you wait'. Lord Krishna replied with a smile 'I love to sit and be at such places'.

"As for the mother much can be said and even that will be too little. The love with which she brings you up has no parallel. So when a man honours his father and mother God says, "I regard it as though I have dwelt amongst them and they have honoured Me". But what do we witness today? The parents are being turned out by their own children. There is a tremendous demand for old age homes today and with the passing of each day it is on the increase. The pain given by others is bearable but the one given by your own children becomes difficult to bear. Priti, you know the story of Mansoor?"

Priti replied in the negative and begged of Vadvani to tell her what happened in Mansoor's life.

Vadvani began, "Mansoor was punished for believing in what he considered to be the truth and not what the king asked him to believe in. The king made him stand in the middle of the main market and ordered that one person from each family must come out and throw a stone at him. But Mansoor stood firm and steady with no sign of pain caused to him. It was noticed that his dear friend had not come out, so a man quickly ran and

brought him out of his house. Not to hurt him, the friend put a few flowers in a piece of cloth and threw it at him. As soon as it touched his body he started weeping and big tears rolled out on his cheeks. The friend was surprised, came near him and asked, "Well I took all care not to hurt you, even then you cried, while you were so calm and quiet as others hurt you so badly".
Mansoor replied, "When others threw stones at me they could only hurt my body. I could bear that but when you joined them, one who knew me so well, and we loved each other so much, what you threw crossed my body and broke my heart and the pain thus caused was so immense that tears naturally rolled out on my cheeks."
"So Priti what really hurts you deeply is when stones come from your own. What can be more painful to the parents then when their own children abuse them, talk ill of them and turn them out of the house! Do you think a home is ever blessed where the children have not learnt to respect their own parents? Give a serious thought to it".
Priti's eyes became wet as she heard all this. She got up and said, "Thank you madam, all this is enough for me to ponder on and has given me food for thought." They parted.

Priti realised that truth was coming to her in a very strange and interesting manner. She felt something was hitting her heart and mind both. She heard Vadvani in rapt attention and pondered over those thoughts when she was alone. Next time when she sat with her, she commented "I believe that you need to have a lot of money to be happy".

"Well" Vadvani spoke thoughtfully, "Yes, we do need some money to keep ourselves going. But if you feel that it is money that is the cause of happiness, I do not agree with you".

"See our next door neighbour, madam", said Priti "They have lot of money so they have no problems. They not only live comfortably, but have great fun in life".

Vadvani replied, "if your happiness depends on money, you can never be happy with yourself. Wealth alone is the root cause of niggardliness, boastfulness, pride, fear and anxiety. I feel what you actually need is contentment in what you have and rejoicing in the things as they are. But those running after money realize their mistake when they end up in grief and disaster. In nature's economy, the currency is life and not money. Enjoy the moments of life by being content with whatever you have.

"Someone's success story cannot become yours, if you try to imitate without having his expertise. I remember myself joining hands with my son who was desirous to become rich by doing business as his friends had. We all felt that soon we would earn a lot of money and then be really happy. After my husband's retirement, he put all his money that he got from the government, in this business. The little that I was earning we readily put in there. Lacking the expertise of how one should go about in business we soon landed in distress and disaster losing even all that we had. Desiring to be happy after becoming rich we lost all that we had and passed the days in anxiety paying off those from whom we had borrowed and lost all peace because of the criminal cases heaped on us by the government.

I then learnt that we need to content with whatever we possess. If your happiness depends on possessing lot of money, then you can never be happy. You need to rejoice in things as they are. If you feel you have the expertise to change your position, definitely go ahead and work towards it, but otherwise accept whatever you have and be happy. Contentment leads to a very important feature in one's life. And that is to enjoy the present moments of your life as you are passing through it. The past is over and it will be useless to keep on thinking about it. The future is still to come: why worry about it? Both ways you are losing the lovely moments of the present which you can and need to enjoy. I remember a lawyer friend of mine who was ever busy making money for his future. He charged for his services but also charged even if he talked giving his opinion. Every act of his concentrated on money and thought for the future. His child saw all this and was unhappy that his dad was never with him. He took out some small amount out of his pocket money and saved it in a small tin box. Then he went to his father and said, 'Here is some money I have saved. As you charge for your time, this is your fee, Papa. I request you to be present for just half an hour on my birthday party. This is all that I want from you at my birthday'. Tears came in the child's eyes as he put forward the little tin box with his tiny hands. Work is essential but equally essential is to enjoy the present moments of life. Sing the song of life by enjoying the present moments of your life and not always be looking for the future. The moments that you are losing will never come back. There is neither past nor future. There is only the present. What we do is to fret for the past or are anxious about the future.

Intelligent people only deal with the present. This is what Chanakya told us. The present, if you think seriously, is a gift from the Divine. It needs to be enjoyed. The life as it is happening needs to be appreciated, needs to be enjoyed. You must understand the importance of the present. Enjoy the present and that is life. A musician was given ten minutes to sing on the stage. He came and kept on preparing himself to sing, by tuning his guitar, by sitting in a proper way, then clearing his throat and so on. The time was over and he was asked to come down. He wasted his time in preparing and never sang. Let your life not be passed in preparing yourself for the future, never enjoying the music of life that is there in the present".

Priti spoke a little seriously "Your reflections on life are so real and connected so closely to day to day life that I myself get into a reflecting mood. I always look forward to sit with you and listen to you. My other neighbours wonder why I so much love your company. They can never understand the treasure that I get from you.
"Priti I may be right or wrong but I tell you what I feel about life" replied Vadvani.
"Madam I am really thankful to you and wish to hear more from you" said Priti
"I have some urgent work to do, we shall talk about what matters in life when we have time to sit together again". Vadvani got up and went inside.

Priti met Vadvani many times, but every time she postponed telling about her reflections for the next turn. This time Priti, presuming that she will do the same, began by saying,

"This time I must hear from you your reflections on life as you promised long back. Postponing every time for the morrow is not good. While we postpone, life speeds away. We do not know what the morrow brings for us".
"You have become very intelligent in your perceptions" said Vadvani smiling.
"It is the result of your company" was a quick response from Priti.

Vadvani began continuing her talk on the topic she had left last time. "Priti I am reminded of a man who though placed in the best of circumstances always said, "I am under great distress". Whenever I told him "I can see that you are really happy" he would look at me, with a strange expression on his face, and would soon qualify, "You see Vadvani I will be happy when I get into a good job for which I am preparing at this moment'. Luckily he succeeded and got what he wanted. I said 'You must be very happy now'. Quick came a reply, 'Not at all' I was surprised and asked 'But why now'? He replied with a long face again, 'You see I will be happy when the problem of getting married to a good girl is over". When the problem was over and he got married to a pretty, understanding girl and I asked him, 'You must be happy now' I got the same answer. In fact every time I met him he was always under some false distress, always looking for the future, never ever enjoying the present moments of his life, in which he was so fortunate, always worried about the future. He lost the treasure of his life, the happiness that could have been his, when last time, and it was after many years, I found him standing before an old age home. "How are you here"? I asked him in surprise. He narrated his story of how he was turned out of the house by his own son. I was quiet for then he was in real distress. You see Priti, he was always postponing to look for happiness in the future, never living in the present moments of his life as he was passing through. Time does not wait for anyone. Life speeds away as we keep on postponing. Those who postpone do infinit harm to themselves. Such persons do not live but are only anxiously looking for the future in which they presume they will be happy. Who knows what tomorrow may bring? Enjoy life as you are passing through it. If your happiness depends only on postponing and looking for the morrow to be happy you are making a grave mistake. Take life as it is, enjoy the present. Live in these happy moments of today and feel good about it".

Priti responded quickly, "Exactly, madam, that is why I insist on you to pass on your reflections about life to me here and now and not keep on postponing for tomorrow". They then had a hearty laugh together. Vadvani commented sweetly, "I sometimes forget to implement my own conclusions on life". Priti took no time to pose a few questions on which she wanted Vadvani's reflections and begged of her that there be no more carrying over to the 'next time we are together'. Vadvani replied calmly "If I told you every thing in one sitting you will get so highly confused that you will not be able to arrive at any conclusion for yourself. I am taking one point at a time so that I can impress something on your mind and heart".

"Yes, madam, I get your point. But today please begin by telling me what are the essentials in life that we must cultivate within us to make life going".

"Yes, Priti, I have given importance a to few things in life that I practiced and found that life becomes not only easy but also enjoyable. It is entirely my point of view with which you may agree or disagree. Most important is to have a positive attitude in life. So let me talk to you about this".

"While talking about creating a positive attitude within us, I would say, what you need is to stand firm, determined to make your mind strong. Try to pray to the Divine every day 'Lord give me new mind, new vision, new thoughts new things to make me new". Change your thoughts. Do not let those thoughts enter your mind that put you down. Your life is nothing but your thoughts. So make all out efforts to rise high in your thoughts. Your value rises with new things. Make yourself strong to rise up with positive thoughts. Many of us fear death. But why? It is an inevitable destiny for all. In death soul merges with Parmatma, rejoice in that. Death is there because there is life. Accept the will of the Lord. In fact as someone said rightly, 'death is the privilege of men who live life positively'. Have new experiences and thus increase your value. Pray for the strength like the sun that lights all. Mental attitude should be there to do work. Small works do not make you small. Fulfill your worldly duties towards family, society and religion. Do not ever allow those thoughts enter your mind that make you feel small.

"Avoid negativity in life and learn to be positive. Life with a positive attitude will give you a determination to fight in all the difficult situations. You will make your life short if you suffer from fears all the time. Learn to live a life, something precious that is given to you. Put your hand on your heart and begin the day by closing your eyes, offering your gratitude to One who has given this life to live, laugh, and meditate in silence as to what is right and what is wrong for you. I see you wondering at the heights of the mountains, at the huge waves of the fast running waters but you fail to wonder at the most wonderful thing that is you, yourself. You are apt to face disastrous situations in your life. If tears come in your eyes, offer them to Him for none will bother about those tears. Wipe them yourself, dry your eyes and move ahead with a new vision, new strength, with steadfastness and without negativity in life.

"Learn to be strong. Do not become a parrot that happily makes the golden cage its home, for he can never feel the vastness of the sky. A person who has no faith in himself will never achieve anything in life. Your faith in yourself ought to be the outcome of faith in God. A life lived in fear will be most uncomfortable. You need not become a slave to your comforts, to your surroundings and to your possessions; else you become a parrot of the golden cage that has no history. Get out of your cage and live a new life. Fly high and listen to your conscience and act according to your inward strength. Your courage, which I am sure you have, will make you win even in the worst situation. You may be defeated but never fear defeats. Your astrologer will warn you that the worst time awaits you. Tell him, "You are wrong and I do not believe you". Let him not overpower you. It is your faith in yourself, your steadfastness, your vision that will succeed. Remember your thoughts will take you up and down. Your desire to go up will definitely take you up. But if your thoughts are otherwise, you will definitely be doomed.

"A dynamite inventor was called 'a destroyer of the world', 'a messenger of death' and was always associated with such epithets. He felt very sad and so he started giving out prizes for doing good work. He was then revered by all and the epithets soon changed. He was then called 'a promoter of good', 'encouragement for many'. Do something good by which you will be remembered. Do something good to your circle, however small it may be. To bring change in society you need to come out. If you try to do even a little, it is worthwhile. Do not keep on blowing horn sitting in the car. Create a mental attitude of satisfaction in what you have, only then it will be possible for you to move on. Do something good to your circle, however small it may be, to be remembered later on. Leave this world in such a manner that you are remembered by your good deeds.

"Give thanks to God that He gave you a lot. Remember Him in your prayers. Prayer without feeling has no meaning. There were many small people who lifted themselves, leaving far behind them very learned pandits that uttered high sounding 'mantras' and had great knowledge. What does God need? He has all. Have you reached your aim by visiting temples? No. I would ask you to attach your mind with Him. This has to be reached inwardly. Join your hands for Him. It is your heart now that must speak out. You forget the formalities but have a strong feeling of nearness to Him and whatever you do is a prayer. Your prayers ought to be "Oh Lord, You never sleep, You are always awake looking after us. Give me a little bit of your strength so that I am always awake to do good and to think high".

Prayer is learnt in the beginning but then it begins to come from within and then it gives you the strength to walk on the path of goodness. Even a small action towards good matters. You are only a clay vessel that can break any time, but in life after life if you do good you will finally reach the top".
Vadvani was quiet for sometime and then she said "I have spoken for a long time, I have to go to the doctor so I will speak when we meet again".

Priti got up and said, "I shall eagerly look for that time". They parted. In the meantime Priti went to meet her sister Punita residing in Bombay, who was highly impressed by Vadvani's life and her chain of thoughts. She was eager to meet this very interesting personality. So she came along to Delhi with her sister and went to meet Vadvani.
"This is my sister Punita" Priti introduced her to Vadvani "who is impressed by your ideas and wanted to meet you. She has come with me to see you and hear from you what more you have to tell us".

Vadvani smiled and replied "I am nothing, only Priti gives high regards to me and broadly agrees with what I say. I on my part too like to sit with her because elders must pass on to the young ones some of the truths that they have felt strongly. In fact that is what I have been doing as a teacher. I feel there ought to be a constant close contact of the young with the old for the benefit of both. I always emphasise those ideas that I believe to be truths of life. I also tell her what I have heard from others and as I have followed those ideas I have found myself in a state of quiet satisfaction".

Punita replied, "Yes madam, even I have been much impressed by how you have courageously fought in your life and arrived at conclusions that can also help us in making our lives better. I consider my self lucky to sit by your side and hear you".

Vadvani then spoke as she smiled, "I am no sage or a philosopher but I feel very strongly that love needs to be the foundation of our lives. It needs to come from within. This is possible only after you have learnt to forget a little of yourself. We need to try to live with a feeling of nearness to the Divine, only then we will be in a state of happiness. We are all the children of the same Father, coming from the same place. Why then get divided as to be at the throats of each other? Definitely we have varied problems and varied thoughts. But so what? We are all one. Do not create fear in the hearts of others. Do not learn to stab in the back of the other. The example of a scarecrow strikes me. You know it is standing in the middle of a field extending its hands to create fear in the hearts of the birds and doing so it forgets itself. Once someone asked the scarecrow, "You keep on extending your hands, bearing all types of weather rains, heat, cold and what not and you never get tired". The scarecrow replied, "Oh! I find so much of pleasure in doing so that I completely forget myself". The question arises, are we scarecrows? Are we those who are interested in creating fear in the hearts of others? Try to think who we are and then behave accordingly. We need to save ourselves from falling low. No one can help us but only we ourselves can. And I repeat no one can and no one may. We ourselves must walk the path. Do something good for others. We need to put our hands out only to help and not to hurt".

Punita listening to Vadvani said thoughtfully "We are always deeply involved in our own turmoil that we hardly get time to think of others".
Vadvani interrupted "Why give all your time to your distress? Think of others. Give, if only a little time to their difficulties and help them out. This will provide you with a lot of strength and courage within yourself. Try this. Those given to too much ease and rest and confined to themselves find it difficult to face life and its problems. Distress is something very important in life. Distress and an ability to face it bravely, give you the courage to move on in life easily. You slipped once, twice or thrice. So what? It does not matter. All that you need is to keep on moving. Learn to face your problems with ease and with confidence. Let nothing pull your spirits down. Learn to climb the steps of your life with a broad smile on your face. It is only then that you will learn to get the courage to face the worst that can happen to you. Happiness needs to be found in the small happenings of day to day life. Search the need of your life yourself. It cannot be borrowed. As you proceed in life, be happy. Enjoy whatever you have and be satisfied. Anger, disgust and frustration are habits that you need to keep away. Avoid such habits. Instead learn to smile. Learn to help others. It will make your life so easy.

Priti said, "Madam, your reflections coming from what you have gone through yourself in life really touch the heart and mind both and convincingly show the path that we need to follow".

Punita intervened and said "But I would like to know as to whom you would place the highest in your list of good men, for we meet with all types of persons in our day to day life".
Vadvani, "It is difficult to answer your question straight off. It is the sum total in a person that gives him a place in the list as to where he stands. But if you ask my opinion, there are certain qualities that one needs to cultivate in him self. One must keep a balance in life. Anything you do, you need to keep a balance, else it is likely to create havoc. While rising high in life, remember the Lord whose blessings are behind it. Remember pride of any type is bad. Pride over beauty, pride over possession, pride over wealth, or pride over wisdom will be disastrous for you. Do not begin to think too highly of yourself if you have any of these. Also you on your part do not begin to think you are right and others are wrong. You need to be humble and remember humility always pays. Always remember God. Offer your gratitude to Him, only then you will feel that inside you a sweet flower is growing and this is the flower of humility. The highest is one who dedicates himself to do good to others. Where there is no love and compassion, you need not enter. You need to act so that the smiles come on the face of others. Let your eyes become moist when you see the tears in the eyes of others. In order to earn or to rise never do it at the cost of others. Nothing can be more hateful than this. Try to help, at least do not pull down others. At least do not be guided by what they say 'let us be smart'.

Another thing to remember is that we need to expand our limits. A candle or a 'deep' if put on a higher level gives light to a larger area than if put on the ground. Each one of us wants to rise, but obstructions on the path pull the person down. I would suggest that you need to have a single vision after which you must go. Go after it with all the strength at your command. Having too many visions, and running after many, you may not succeed even in one. If you dig at many places for the water to come out, you will fail. But if you keep on digging at one place the water is bound to come out. Try to pick up knowledge from all men and from the smallest events as you go about. Newton learnt the law of gravitation from a very small and simple event in his life.

"My last query to you madam, before I leave for Bombay" requested Parnita "is your promise to tell me how to have 'Anand' in an ordinary life."

Vadvani sat down, and then spoke thoughtfully with a lovely smile on her face.

"Love and music come from within. It is a state that comes after you learn to forget yourself. You need to get out of your selfishness and that is by not confining to your small family, and to yourself, a very limited circle. Self needs should be subdued. To bring this change, create a mental attitude of satisfaction in what you have. It is only then that you can move out of yourself. Do good to others and their happiness is sure to give you immense happiness. Happiness is nothing but living every minute with love and compassion. It is like a perfume you pour on others but you are sure to get some on yourself. Happiness is not a ready made formula; it comes from your actions. You need to love those around you and not only yourself. And as

ParamHans points out, 'A happy man attracts into his body a great supply of 'universal life energy' that keeps him away from distress and diseases'.

"Learn to smile to make your life easy in the worst of circumstances. Develop an attitude of gratitude and give thanks for every thing that happens in your life, knowing well that every step forward is a step towards achieving something bigger and better than your current situation. You asked me where is 'Anand' to be found. Remember you have come from Anand and can well find it in the small happenings of your life. Learn to be happy in whatever you have and don't think that happiness will come tomorrow when your expectations make you imagine that you will have more. What if those expectations do not come true? You are apt to land up in tensions and frustrations. Face all the events of your life bravely and with a smile on your face. You need to find Anand in the small happenings of your day to day life. Balance your life in searching for happiness in the daily happenings, in the little things you have and the little ways that you can help others. Search the need of your life yourself. It cannot be borrowed. As you proceed in life experience 'Anand' in every moment. Anger and frustration are not good for your health. You will not be punished but finished by such habits Why then have them? Instead instill in yourself the habit to smile. It will be so easy to proceed in life.

"A procession of men that ran to safer places from that of disaster took on the head their best. The one who carried jewelry, gold and silver walked with expanded

chest, those who followed went according to their possessions, but at the end walked a great philosopher with torn clothes, with nothing to carry yet with expanded chest. All laughed at him and commented, "Look at that fool. He has nothing to possess, not even proper clothes, yet he is walking with expanded chest more than the best".
The man very humbly replied
"I have that which I will never lose my Anand, my smile".

"The one lesson that you need to learn is to smile under the worst condition. Your thoughts must be high. Depression at all cost must be avoided. If you have learnt to smile as you proceed in life, you have learnt the right lesson. Depressive thoughts at all cost must always be avoided. If ever such thoughts enter your mind change them immediately. Depression is a disease that finishes a life. Do not allow ever such thoughts to overpower you. Your thoughts must always be high to bring a charming smile on your face. If depressive thoughts ever disturb you throw them into a dustbin. There should not be a second thought on this. Change the low into high. Leave all that worries you, this very moment. Enthusiasm, courage and smiles are the things you need. Sit alone, be with God and think how you need to stand in life. Definitely not as one who has lost all enthusiasm to live. Happiness and troubles follow each other for this is what life means. Take them in your stride and walk the path of life with a head held high and a winning smile on your face. Do not be an introvert. Be an extrovert who smiles, and laughs, as he crosses the path of life, extending his hand to any that needs it.

"You need to remember one thing that is very important for you. Never for a moment forget One who is always watching you with compassion. Do not rush to the mountains or to the temples to search Him. He has vacated these places for He got disgusted and disgruntled with people thronging Him always complaining of their ills. He pondered upon places where He could hide Himself from this mad rush. After much discussion, He thought of a place where men do not go. He ran and hid Himself there. Can you guess that place? He ran and hid himself in the hearts of men, a place where we never go. So you have to search Him there where He is sitting and looking at you, waiting for you eagerly, smiling that you are not reaching Him. You are the one that He loves the most. He wants you to have faith in Him, confidence in yourself and a smile for all as you walk the path of your life.

"Priti, I know well that I am a category in myself because my approach to the problem of life is quite different from many. I am not against what you think about your problems and how you need to look at life. But I am against principles that may be thrust forcibly on me or for on any one. I am in full agreement with the writer who says:

"To the question of your life, you are the answer and to the problem of your life, you are the solution".

□□□